THE MEURSAULT INVESTIGATION

The Meursault Investigation

Kamel Daoud

TRANSLATED FROM THE FRENCH
BY JOHN CULLEN

OTHER PRESS

NEW YORK

Originally published in French as *Meursault, contre-enquête* by Éditions Barzakh
in Algeria in 2013, and by Actes Sud in France in 2014.

Translation copyright © Other Press, 2015

An excerpt from this novel was first published in the April 6, 2015 issue of *The New Yorker*.

The author has quoted and occasionally adapted certain passages from *The Stranger*
by Albert Camus, translated by Matthew Ward (New York: Alfred A. Knopf, 1988).
The lyrics on pages 55–56 are from "Malou Khouya" by Khaled.

Production editor: Yvonne E. Cárdenas
Text designer: Julie Fry
This book was set in Fournier.

10 9 8 7 6 5 4 3 2 1

Library of Congress Cataloging-in-Publication Data
Daoud, Kamel.
  [Meursault, contre-enquête. English]
  The Meursault investigation / Kamel Daoud ; translated by John Cullen.
    pages cm
  ISBN 978-1-59051-751-2 (paperback) — ISBN 978-1-59051-752-9 (e-book)
  1. Arabs—Fiction. 2. Camus, Albert, 1913–1960. Étranger—Fiction. 3. Algeria—Fiction.
4. Psychological fiction. 5. Political fiction. I. Cullen, John, 1942– translator. II. Title.

  PQ3989.3.D365M4813 2015
  843'.92—dc23

                                                    2015010736

For Aïda.

For Ikbel.

My open eyes.

The hour of crime does not strike at the same time for every people. This explains the permanence of history.

—E. M. CIORAN
Syllogismes de l'amertume

I

Mama's still alive today.

She doesn't say anything now, but there are many tales she could tell. Unlike me: I've rehashed this story in my head so often, I almost can't remember it anymore.

I mean, it goes back more than half a century. It happened, and everyone talked about it. People still do, but they mention only one dead man, they feel no compunction about doing that, even though there were two of them, two dead men. Yes, two. Why does the other one get left out? Well, the original guy was such a good storyteller, he managed to make people forget his crime, whereas the other one was a poor illiterate God created apparently for the sole purpose of taking a bullet and returning to dust—an anonymous person who didn't even have the time to be given a name.

I'll tell you this up front: The other dead man, the murder victim, was my brother. There's nothing left of him. There's only me, left to speak in his place, sitting in this bar, waiting for condolences no one's ever going to offer. Laugh if you want, but this is more or less my mission: I peddle offstage silence, trying to sell my story while the theater empties out. As a matter of fact, that's the reason why I've learned to speak this language, and to write it too: so I can speak in the place of a dead man, so I can finish his sentences for him. The murderer got famous, and his story's too well written for me to get any ideas about imitating him. He wrote in his own language. Therefore I'm going to do what was done in this country after Independence: I'm going to take the stones from the old houses the colonists left behind, remove them one by one, and build my own house, my own language. The murderer's words and expressions are my *unclaimed goods*. Besides, the country's littered with words that don't belong to anyone anymore. You see them on the façades of old stores, in yellowing books, on people's faces, or transformed by the strange creole decolonization produces.

So it's been quite some time since the murderer died, and much too long since my brother ceased to exist for everyone but me. I know, you're eager to ask the type of questions I hate, but please listen to me instead, please give me your attention, and by and by you'll understand. This is no normal story. It's a story that begins at the end and goes back to the beginning. Yes, like a school of salmon swimming upstream. I'm sure you're like everyone else, you've read the tale as told by the man who wrote it. He writes so well that his words are like precious stones, jewels cut with the utmost precision. A man very strict about shades of meaning, your hero was; he practically required them to be mathematical. Endless calculations, based on gems and minerals. Have you seen the way he writes? He's writing about a gunshot, and he makes it sound like poetry! His world is clean, clear, exact, honed by morning sunlight, enhanced with fragrances and horizons. The only shadow is cast by "the Arabs," blurred, incongruous objects left over from "days gone by," like ghosts, with no language except the sound of a flute. I tell myself he must have been fed up with wandering around in circles in a country that wanted nothing to do with him, whether dead or alive. The murder he committed seems like the act of a disappointed lover unable to possess the land he loves. How he must have suffered, poor man! To be the child of a place that never gave you birth...

I too have read his version of the facts. Like you and millions of others. And everyone got the picture, right from the start: *He* had a man's name; my brother had the name of an incident. He could have called him "Two P.M.," like that other writer who called his black man "Friday." An hour of the day instead of a day of the week. Two in the afternoon, that's good. *Zujj* in Algerian Arabic, two, the pair, him and me, the unlikeliest twins, somehow, for those who know the story of the story. A brief Arab, technically ephemeral, who lived for two hours and has died incessantly for seventy years, long after his funeral. It's like my brother Zujj has been kept under glass. And even though he was a murder victim, he's always given some vague designation, complete with reference to the two hands of a clock, over and over again, so that he replays his own death, killed by a bullet fired by a Frenchman who just didn't know what to do with his day and with the rest of the world, which he carried on his back.

And again! Whenever I go over this story in my head, I get angry — at least, I do whenever I have the strength. So the Frenchman plays the dead man and goes on and on about how he lost his mother, and then about how he lost his body in the sun, and then about how he lost a girlfriend's body, and then about how he went to church and

3

discovered that his God had deserted the human body, and then about how he sat up with his mother's corpse and his own, et cetera. Good God, how can you kill someone and then take even his own death away from him? My brother was the one who got shot, not him! It was Musa, not Meursault, see? There's something I find stunning, and it's that nobody — not even after Independence — nobody at all ever tried to find out what the victim's name was, or where he lived, or what family he came from, or whether he had children. Nobody. Everyone was knocked out by the perfect prose, by language capable of giving air facets like diamonds, and everyone declared their empathy with the murderer's solitude and offered him their most learned condolences. Who knows Musa's name today? Who knows what river carried him to the sea, which he had to cross on foot, alone, without his people, without a magic staff? Who knows whether Musa had a gun, a philosophy, or a sunstroke?

Who was Musa? He was my brother. That's what I'm getting at. I want to tell you the story Musa was never able to tell. When you opened the door of this bar, you opened a grave, my young friend. Do you happen to have the book in your schoolbag there? Good. Play the disciple and read me the first page or so...

So. Did you understand? No? I'll explain it to you. After his mother dies, this man, this murderer, finds himself without a country and falls into idleness and absurdity. He's a Robinson Crusoe who thinks he can change his destiny by killing his Friday but instead discovers he's trapped on an island and starts banging on like a self-indulgent parrot. "Poor Meursault, where are you?"

4

Shout out those words a few times and they'll seem less ridiculous, I promise. And I'm asking that question for your sake. *I* know the book by heart, I can recite it to you like the Koran. That story—a corpse wrote it, not a writer. You can tell by the way he suffers from the sun and gets dazzled by colors and has no opinion on anything except the sun, the sea, and the surrounding rocks. From the very beginning, you can sense that he's looking for my brother. And in fact, he seeks him out, not so much to meet him as to never have to. What hurts me every time I think about it is that he killed him by passing over him, not by shooting him. You know, his crime is majestically nonchalant. It made any subsequent attempt to present my brother as a *shahid*, a martyr, impossible. The martyr came too long after the murder. In the interval, my brother rotted in his grave and the book obtained its well-known success. And afterward, therefore, everybody bent over backward to prove there was no murder, just sunstroke.

Ha, ha! What are you drinking? In these parts, you get offered the best liquors after your death, not before. And that's religion, my brother. Drink up—in a few years, after the end of the world, the only bar still open will be in Paradise.

I'm going to outline the story before I tell it to you. A man who knows how to write kills an Arab who, on the day he dies, doesn't even have a name, as if he'd hung it on a nail somewhere before stepping onto the stage. Then the man begins to explain that his act was the fault of a God who doesn't exist and that he did it because of what he'd just realized in the sun and because the sea salt

5

obliged him to shut his eyes. All of a sudden, the murder is a deed committed with absolute impunity and wasn't a crime anyway because there's no law between noon and two o'clock, between him and Zujj, between Meursault and Musa. And for seventy years now, everyone has joined in to disappear the victim's body quickly and turn the place where the murder was committed into an intangible museum. What does "Meursault" mean? *Meurt seul*, dies alone? *Meurt sot*, dies a fool? Never dies? My poor brother had no say in this story. And that's where you go wrong, you and all your predecessors. The absurd is what my brother and I carry on our backs or in the bowels of our land, not what the other was or did. Please understand me, I'm not speaking in either sorrow or anger. I'm not even going to play the mourner. It's just that…it's just what? I don't know. I think I'd just like justice to be done. That may seem ridiculous at my age…But I swear it's true. I don't mean the justice of the courts, I mean the justice that comes when *the scales are balanced*. And I've got another reason besides: I want to pass away without being pursued by a ghost. I think I can guess why people write true stories. Not to make themselves famous but to make themselves more invisible, and all the while clamoring for a piece of the world's true core.

Drink up and look out the window—you'd think this country was an aquarium. Right, right, but it's your fault too, my friend; your curiosity provokes me. I've been waiting for you for years, and if I can't write my book, at least I can tell you the story, can't I? A man who's drinking is always dreaming about a man who'll listen. That's today's bit of wisdom, write it down in your notebook…

It's simple: The story we're talking about should be rewritten, in the same language, but from right to left. That is, starting when the Arab's body was still alive, going down the narrow streets that led to his demise, giving him a name, right up until the bullet hit him. So one reason for learning this language was to tell this story for my brother, the friend of the sun. Seems unlikely to you? You're wrong. I had to find the response nobody wanted to give me when I needed it. You drink a language, you speak a language, and one day it owns you; and from then on, it falls into the habit of grasping things in your place, it takes over your mouth like a lover's voracious kiss. I knew someone who learned to write in French because one day his illiterate father received a telegram no one could decipher. This was in the days when your hero was still alive and the colonists were still running the show. The telegram lay rotting in this fellow's pocket for a week before somebody read it to him. In three lines, it informed him of his mother's death, somewhere deep in the treeless country. He told me, "I learned to write for my father, and I learned to write so that such a thing could never happen again. I'll never forget his anger with himself, and his eyes begging me to help him." Basically, my reason's the same as his. Well, go on, read some more, even if the whole thing's written in my head. Every night, my brother Musa, alias Zujj, arises from the Realm of the Dead and pulls my beard and cries, "Oh my brother Harun, why did you let this happen? I'm not a sacrificial lamb, damn it, I'm your brother!" Go on, read!

Let's be clear from the start: There were just two siblings, my brother and me. We didn't have a sister, much less a slutty one, as your hero suggested in his book. Musa was my older brother, his head seemed to strike the clouds. He was quite tall, yes, and his body was thin and knotty from hunger and the strength anger gives. He had an angular face, big hands that protected me, and hard eyes because our ancestors lost their land. But when I think about it, I believe he already loved us then the way the dead do, with a look in his eyes that came from the hereafter and with no useless words. I don't have many pictures of him in my head, but I want to describe them to you carefully. For example, the day he came home early from the neighborhood market, or maybe from the port, where he worked as a porter and handyman, toting, dragging, lifting, sweating. Anyway, that day he came across me while I was playing with an old tire, and he put me on his shoulders and told me to hold on to his ears, as if his head were a steering wheel. I remember how ecstatic I felt while he rolled the tire along and made a sound like a motor. His smell comes back to me too, a persistent mingling of rotten vegetables, sweat, muscles, and breath. Another picture in my memory is from the day of Eid one year. He'd given me a hiding the day before for some stupid thing I'd done and now we were both embarrassed. It was a day of forgiveness, he was supposed to kiss me, but I didn't want him to lose face and lower himself by apologizing to me, not even in God's name. I also remember his gift for immobility, the way he'd stand stock-still on the threshold of our house, facing the neighbors' wall, holding a cigarette and the cup of black coffee our mother would bring him.

Our father had disappeared ages before, reduced to fragments by the rumors of people who claimed to have run into him in France, and only Musa could hear his voice. He'd give Musa commands in his dreams, and Musa would relay them to us. My brother had seen him again only once since he'd left, and from such a distance that he wasn't really sure it was him anyway. As a child, I knew how to distinguish the days with rumors from the days without. When my brother Musa would hear people talk about my father, he'd come home, all feverish gestures and burning eyes, and then he and Mama would have long, whispered conversations that always ended in heated arguments. I was excluded from those, but I got the gist: For some obscure reason, my brother held a grudge against Mama, and she defended herself in a way that was even more obscure. Those were unsettling days and nights, filled with anger, and I recall my panic at the idea that Musa might leave us too. But he'd always return at dawn, drunk, oddly proud of his rebellion, seemingly endowed with renewed strength. Then my brother Musa would sober up and fade away. All he wanted to do was sleep, and so my mother would get him under her control again. I've got some pictures in my head, they're all I can offer you. A cup of coffee, some cigarette butts, his espadrilles, Mama crying and then recovering very quickly to smile at a neighbor who'd come to borrow some tea or spices, moving from distress to courtesy so fast it made me doubt her sincerity, young as I was. Everything revolved around Musa, and Musa revolved around our father, whom I never knew and who left me nothing but our family name. Do you know what we were called in those days? *Uled el-assas*, the sons of the guardian. Of the watchman, to be more precise. My father worked as

9

a night watchman in a factory where they made I don't know what. One night, he disappeared. And that's all. That's the story I got. It happened in the 1930s, right after I was born. That's why I always imagine him gloomy, wrapped up in a coat or a black djellaba, crouching in some dim corner, and silent, without so much as a single answer for me.

So Musa was a simple god, a god of few words. His thick beard and strong arms made him seem like a giant who could have wrung the neck of any soldier in any ancient pharaoh's army. Which explains why, on the day when we learned of his death and the circumstances surrounding it, I didn't feel sad or angry at first; instead I felt disappointed and offended, as if someone had insulted me. My brother Musa was capable of parting the sea, and yet he died in insignificance, like a common bit player, on a beach that today has disappeared, close to the waves that should have made him famous forever!

I almost never wept for him, I just stopped looking at the sky the way I used to. Moreover, in later years, I didn't even fight in the War of Liberation. I knew it was won in advance, from the moment when a member of my family was killed because someone felt lethargic from too much sun. As soon as I learned to read and write, everything became clear to me: I had my mother, while Meursault had lost his. He killed, but I knew it was really a way of committing suicide. Now, it's true that I reached those conclusions before the scenery got shifted and the roles reversed. Before I realized how alike we were, he and I, imprisoned in the same cell, shut up out of sight in a place where bodies were nothing but costumes.

And so the story of this murder doesn't begin with the famous sentence "Maman died today" but with words no one has ever heard, spoken by my brother Musa to my mother on that last day, right before he went out: "I'll be home earlier than usual." It was a day, as I recall, *without*. Remember what I told you about my world and its binary calendar: the days *with* rumors about my father, and the days *without*, which Musa dedicated to smoking, arguing with Mama, and looking at me like a piece of furniture requiring nourishment. In reality, as I now realize, I did what Musa had done; he'd replaced my father, and I replaced my brother. But wait, I'm lying to you about that, just as for a long time I lied to myself. The truth is that Independence only pushed people on both sides to switch roles. We were the ghosts in this country when the settlers were exploiting it and bestowing on it their church bells and cypress trees and swans. And today? Well, it's just the opposite! They come back sometimes, holding their descendants' hands on trips organized for pieds-noirs or for people affected by their parents' nostalgia, trying to find a street or a house or a tree with initials carved in its trunk. I recently saw a group of French tourists standing in front of a tobacco shop at the airport. Like discreet, mute specters, they watched us — us Arabs — in silence, as if we were nothing but stones or dead trees. Nevertheless, that's all over now. That's what their silence said.

I maintain that when you're investigating a crime, you must keep in mind its essential elements: Who's the dead man? Who was he? I want you to make a note of my brother's name, because he was the one who was killed in the first place and the one who's still being killed to this day. I insist on that, because otherwise, we may as well part right here. You carry off your book, I'll take up the body, and to each his way. The genealogy I'm talking about is pretty pathetic in any case! I'm the son of the guardian, *uld el-assas*, and the Arab's brother. Here in Oran, you know, people are obsessed with origins. *Uled el-bled*, the real children of the city, of the country. Everyone wants to be this city's only son, the first, the last, the oldest. The bastard's anxiety — sounds like there's some of that rattling around, don't you think? Everyone tries to prove he was the first — him, his father, or his grandfather — to live here. All the others are foreigners, landless peasants ennobled en masse by Independence. I've always wondered why people like that poke about so anxiously in cemeteries. Yes, yes they do. Maybe it's from fear, or from the scramble for property. The first people to have lived here? Confirmed skeptics or recent newcomers call them "the rats." This is a city with its legs spread open toward the sea. Take a look at the port when you walk down toward the old neighborhoods in Sidi El Houari, over on the Calère des Espagnols side. It's like an old whore, nostalgic and chatty. Sometimes I go down to the lush garden on the Promenade de Létang to have a solitary drink and rub shoulders with delinquents. Yes, down there, where you see that strange, dense vegetation, ficuses, conifers, aloes, not to mention palms and other deeply rooted trees, growing up toward the sky as well as down under the earth. Below there's a vast labyrinth of Spanish and Turkish galleries, which I've been able to visit, even though they're usually closed. I saw an astonishing spectacle down there: the roots of centuries-old trees, seen from the inside, so to speak, gigantic, twisting things, like giant, naked, suspended flowers. Go and visit that garden. I love the place, but sometimes when I'm there I detect the scent of a woman's sex, a giant, worn-out one. Which goes a little way toward confirming my obscene vision: This city faces the sea with its legs apart, its thighs spread, from the bay to the high ground where that luxurious, fragrant garden is. It was conceived — or should I say *inseminated*, ha, ha! — by a general, General Létang, in 1847. You absolutely must go and see it — then you'll understand why people here are dying to have famous ancestors. To escape from the evidence.

Have you noted it down? My brother's name was Musa. He had a name. But he'll remain "the Arab" forever. The last on the list, excluded from the inventory that Crusoe of yours made. Strange, isn't it? For centuries, the settler increases his fortune, giving names to whatever he appropriates and taking them away from whatever makes him feel uncomfortable. If he calls my brother "the Arab," it's so he can kill him the way one kills time, by strolling around aimlessly. For your guidance, I'll tell you that for years after Independence, Mama fought to be awarded a pension as the mother of a martyr. As you can imagine, she never got it, and why not, if you please? Because it was impossible to prove the Arab was a son — and a brother. Impossible to prove he existed, even though he was killed in public. Impossible to find and confirm a connection between Musa and Musa, between Musa and himself! How can you tell the world about that when you don't know how to write books? Mama wore herself out for a while in the first few months after

Independence, trying to gather signatures or witnesses, but in vain. Nothing was left of Musa, not even a corpse!

Musa, Musa, Musa…I like to repeat that name from time to time so it doesn't disappear. I insist on that, and I want you to write it in big letters. Half a century after his birth and death, a man has just been given a name. I insist.

No, the first night I always pick up the tab. By the way, what's your name?

II

Hello. Yes, quite a blue sky, it looks like a child's coloring book. Or an answered prayer. I had a bad night. A night of anger. The kind of anger that takes you by the throat, tramples you, pesters you with the same questions, tortures you, tries to force you to make a confession or give up a name. When it's over, you're covered with bruises, like after an interrogation, and you feel like a traitor to boot.

Are you asking me if I want to continue? Yes, of course, at last I have a chance to get this story off my chest!

As a child, I was allowed to hear only one story at night, only one deceptively wonderful tale. It was the story of Musa, my murdered brother, who took a different form every time, according to my mother's mood. In my memory, those nights are associated with rainy winters, with the dim light from the oil lamp in our hovel, and with Mama's murmuring voice. Such nights didn't come often, only when we were short on food, when it was too cold, and maybe, as I believe, when Mama felt even more like a widow than usual. Oh, stories die, you know, and I can't exactly remember anything the poor woman told me, but she knew how to summon her remaining memories of her parents and her family's tribe and what women talked about among themselves. Unlikely things, tales of hand-to-hand combat between Musa, the invisible giant,

15

and the *gaouri*, the *roumi*, the big fat Frenchman, the obese thief of sweat and land. And so in our imagination, my brother Musa was commissioned to perform different tasks: repay a blow, avenge an insult, recover a piece of confiscated land, collect a paycheck. All of a sudden, this legendary Musa acquired a horse and a sword and the aura of a spirit come back from the dead to redress injustice. Ah well, you know how it goes. When he was alive, he already had a reputation as a quick-tempered man with a fondness for impromptu boxing matches. Most of Mama's tales, however, concentrated on chronicling Musa's last day, which was also, in a way, the first day of his immortality. Mama could narrate the events of that day in such staggering detail that it almost came to life. She wouldn't describe a murder and a death, she'd evoke a fantastic transformation, one that turned a simple young man from the poorer quarters of Algiers into an invincible, long-awaited hero, a kind of savior. The versions would change. In some of them, Musa had left the house a little earlier, awakened by a prophetic dream or a terrifying voice that had pronounced his name. In others, he'd answered the call of some friends — *uled el-huma*, sons of the neighborhood — idle young men interested in skirts, cigarettes, and scars. An obscure discussion ensued and resulted in Musa's death. I'm not sure: Mama had a thousand and one stories, and the truth meant little to me at that age. What was most important at those moments was my almost sensual closeness with Mama and our muffled reconciliation in the night to come. The next morning everything was back in its place, my mother in one world and me in another.

What can I tell you, Mr. Investigator, about a crime committed in a book? I don't know what happened on that particular day, in that gruesome summer, between six o'clock in the morning and two in the afternoon, the hour of Musa's death. There we are! Besides, after Musa was killed, nobody came around to question us. There was no serious investigation. I have a hard time remembering what I myself did that day. In the morning, the same neighborhood characters were awake and on the street. Down at one end, we had Tawi and his sons. Tawi was a heavyset fellow. Dragged his bad left leg, had a nagging cough, smoked a lot. And early each morning, it was his habit to step outside and pee on a wall, as blithely as you please. Everybody knew him, because his ritual was so unvarying that he served as a clock; the broken cadence of his footsteps and his cough were the first signs that the new day had arrived in our street. Farther up on the right, there was El-Hajj, alias the pilgrim — which he was by genealogy, not because he'd made the trip to Mecca; El-Hajj was just his real given name. He too was the silent type. His main occupations seemed to be striking his mother and eyeing his neighbors with a permanent air of defiance. On the near corner of the adjacent alley, the Moroccan had a café called El-Blidi. His sons were liars and petty thieves, capable of stealing all the fruit off every possible tree. They'd invented a game: They would throw matches into the sidewalk gutters where the wastewater ran and then follow the course of those matches. They never tired of doing that. I also remember an old woman, Taïbia, big, fat, childless, and very temperamental. Something unsettling and even a little voracious in the way she looked at us — us, other women's offspring — made us giggle nervously. The city, with its thousand alleys, was like a huge geological animal, and we were a little collection of lice on its back.

So on that particular day, nothing unusual. Even Mama, who loved omens and was sensitive to spirits, failed to detect anything abnormal. A routine day, in short — women calling to one another, laundry hung out on the terraces, street vendors. No one could have heard a gunshot from so far away, a shot fired way downtown, on the beach. Not even at the devil's hour, two o'clock on a summer afternoon — the siesta hour. So, Mr. Investigator, I repeat, nothing unusual. Later, of course, I thought about it, and little by little, I concluded that there must be — among the thousand versions Mama offered, among her memory fragments and her still-vivid intuitions — there must be one version truer than the others. In our house in those days, there was something I'm not sure about, something I might call the smell of female rivalry floating in the air, rivalry between Mama and another woman. I never saw her, but Musa carried a trace of her in his voice, in his eyes, and in the way he had of violently rejecting Mama's insinuations. So there was this harem tension, if I can call it that. Like a mute struggle between an exotic perfume and an overly familiar kitchen smell. In our neighborhood, all the women were "sisters." A code of respect prevented the more interesting sorts of romance and reduced the game of seduction to wedding parties or mere glances exchanged while the women hung out the wash on the terraces. For young men of Musa's age, I imagine the neighborhood "sisters" offered the prospect of practically incestuous and not particularly passionate marriages. Now there *were* a few skirt-wearing, firm-breasted Algerian women who shuttled between our world and the world of the *roumis*, down in the French neighborhoods. We brats used to call them whores and stone them with our eyes. They were fascinating targets, because they could promise the pleasures of love without the inevitably of marriage. Those women often inspired violent passions and hateful rivalries, the sort of thing your writer alludes to a few times in his book. However, his version is unfair, because the unseen woman he mentions wasn't Musa's sister. One of his girlfriends, maybe. And there, I've always thought, is where the misunderstanding came from; what in fact was never anything other than a banal score-settling that got out of hand was elevated to a philosophical crime. Musa wanted to save the girl's honor by teaching your hero a lesson, and he protected himself by shooting my brother down in cold blood on a beach. Men in the working-class neighborhoods of Algiers actually did have an exaggerated, grotesque sense of honor. Defend our women and their thighs! I tell myself that after losing their land, their wells, and their livestock, women were all our guys had left. This rather feudal explanation makes me smile too, but do me a favor and think about it. It's not completely crazy. The story in that book of yours comes down to a sudden slipup caused by two great vices: women and laziness. So — and I really think this sometimes — there were indeed some traces of a woman, a scent of jealousy, in Musa's last days. Mama never spoke about it, but in our neighborhood, after the crime, I was often greeted as the heir of some recovered honor, though I could never figure out the reasons why, child that I was. Nevertheless, I knew it! I could feel it. By telling me so many implausible tales and outright lies, Mama eventually aroused my suspicions and put my intuitions in order. I reconstructed the whole thing. Musa's frequent binges in that last period, the scent floating in the air, his proud smile when he ran into his friends, their overly serious, almost comical confabs, the way my brother had of playing with his knife and showing me his tattoos. *Echedda fi Allah*, "God is my support." "March or die" on his right shoulder. "Be quiet" on his left forearm, under a drawing of a broken heart. That was the only book Musa wrote. Shorter than a last sigh, consisting of three sentences on the oldest paper in the world, his own skin. I remember his tattoos the way other people remember their first picture book. Other details? Oh, I don't know, his overalls, his espadrilles, his prophet's beard, and his big hands, which tried to hold on to our father's ghost, and his involvement with a nameless, honorless woman. I'm not sure, Mr. Student Detective.

Ah! The mystery woman! Provided that she existed at all. I know only her first name; at least, I presume it was hers. My brother had spoken it in his sleep that night, the night before his death. Zubida. A sign? Maybe. In any case, the day Mama and I left the neighborhood forever—Mama had decided to get away from Algiers and the sea—I'm sure I saw a woman staring at us. A very intense stare. She was wearing a short skirt and tacky stockings, and it seems to me she'd done her hair like the movie stars in those days: Although she was quite obviously a brunette, her hair was dyed blond. "Zubida forever," ha, ha! Maybe my brother had those words tattooed somewhere on his body as well, I don't know for sure. But I *am* sure it was her that day. It was early in the morning. We were setting out, Mama and I, leaving the house for good, and there she was, holding a little red purse, staring at us from some distance away. I can still see her lips and her huge eyes, which seemed to be asking us for something. I'm almost certain it was her. At the time, I wanted it to be her and I decided it was, because that enhanced my brother's demise somehow. I needed Musa to have had an excuse and a reason. Without realizing it, and years before I learned to read, I rejected the absurdity of his death, and I needed a story to give him a shroud. Well, then. I pulled Mama by her haik, so she didn't see her. But she must surely have sensed something, because she made a horrible face and spat out a prodigiously vulgar insult. I turned around, but the woman had disappeared. And then we left. I remember the road to Hadjout, lined with fields whose crops weren't destined for us, and the naked sun, and the other travelers on the dusty bus. The oil fumes nauseated me, but I loved the virile, almost comforting roar of the engine, like a kind of father that was snatching us, my mother and me, out of an immense labyrinth made up of buildings, downtrodden people, shantytowns, dirty urchins, aggressive cops, and beaches fatal to Arabs. For the two of us, the city would always be the scene of the crime, or the place where something pure and ancient was lost. Yes, Algiers, in my memory, is a dirty, corrupt creature, a dark, treacherous man-stealer.

So how come I've wound up in a city once again, Oran this time? Good question. Maybe it's self-punishment. Look around a little, here in Oran or elsewhere. It's as though people have a grudge against the city and they've come here to trash it and plunder it, like a kind of foreign country. People treat the city like an old harlot, they insult it, they abuse it, they fling garbage in its face, they never stop comparing it to the pure, wholesome little town it used to be in the old days, but they can't leave it, because it's the only possible escape to the sea and the farthest you can get from the desert. Make a note of that, it's quite good, I think, ha, ha! An old song, a local favorite, has a line that goes, "Beer is Arab and whiskey's Western." Which is wrong, of course. I often amend it when I'm alone: The song is Oranian, the beer's Arab, the whiskey's European, the bartenders are Kabyles, the streets are French, the old porticos are Spanish...and I could go on. I've lived here for several decades now, and I like it fine. The sea's down there, far away, crushed underfoot by the harbor. It won't take anyone away from me and can never reach me.

I'm doing fine, see? It's been years since I've seriously spoken my brother's name, except in my head and in this bar. My countrymen have a habit of calling anybody they don't know "Mohammed," but the name I give everyone is "Musa." That's also our barman's name, you can call him that, it'll make him smile. It's as important to give a dead man a name as it is to name a newborn infant. Yes, it's very important. My brother's name was Musa. On the last day of his life, I was seven years old, and so I don't know any more about him than what I've told you.

I can't quite recall the name of our street in Algiers. All I remember is that Bab-el-Oued was the name of the neighborhood, and the market, and the cemetery. The rest has disappeared from my memory. Algiers still scares me, though. It has nothing to say to me and remembers neither me nor my family. And picture this: One summer, it was 1963, I think, right after Independence, I went back to Algiers, determined to conduct my own investigation. But I barely got out of the train station before I lost my resolve and turned back. It was hot, I felt ridiculous in the suit I was wearing, and everything was going so fast it made me dizzy, too fast for a villager used to the slow cycles of harvests and trees. I immediately turned back. My reason? It's obvious, my young friend. I told myself that if I found our old house again, death would end up finding us, Mama and me. And so would the sea, and injustice. That's pompous, and it sounds like a line that's been rehearsed for a long time, but it's also the truth.

Let's see, let me try to remember exactly...How did we learn of Musa's death? I remember a kind of invisible cloud hovering over our street and angry grown-ups talking loud and gesticulating. At first, Mama told me that a *gaouri* had killed one of the neighbor's sons while he was trying to defend an Arab woman and her honor. Then, during the night, anxiety got inside our house, and I think Mama gradually began to realize the truth. So did I, probably. And then, all of a sudden, I heard this long, low moan, swelling until it became immense, a huge mass of sound that destroyed our furniture and blew our walls apart and then blew up the whole neighborhood and left me all alone.

I remember starting to cry for no reason, just because everyone was looking at me. Mama had disappeared, and I got shoved outside, rejected by something more important than me, absorbed into some kind of collective disaster. Strange, don't you think? I told myself, confusedly, that this might be about my father, that he was definitely dead this time, which made me sob twice as hard. It was a long night; nobody slept. A constant stream of people came in to offer their condolences. The grown-ups spoke to me solemnly. When I couldn't understand what they were telling me, I contented myself with looking at their hard eyes, their shaking hands, and their shabby shoes. When the dawn came, I felt very hungry, and I wound up falling asleep I don't know where. No matter how much I dig around in my memory, I have no recollection at all of that day and the next, except I recall the smell of couscous. The days blurred into a sort of immensely long single day, tall and broad like a deep valley, where I meandered with other solemn kids who were showing me the respect due to my new status as "the hero's brother." That's all I remember. The last day of a man's life doesn't exist. Outside of storybooks, there's no hope, nothing but soap bubbles bursting. That's the best proof of our absurd existence, my dear friend: Nobody's granted a final day, just an accidental interruption in his life.

I'm going home. How about you?

Yes, the barman's name is Musa — in my head, at any rate. And the other one, the one over there, in the back? I've christened him Musa too. But he's got a whole different story, that one. He's older and surely half widowed, or half married. Notice his skin, it's like parchment. He's a former inspector of education in the teaching of the French language. I know him. I don't like to look him in the eye because he's liable to seize the opportunity to get inside my head, make himself comfortable, and tell me the story of his life, jabbering away in my place. I keep my distance from sad people. The two other guys behind me? Same profile. The bars still open in this country are aquariums containing mostly bottom-feeders, weighed down and scraping along. You come here when you want to escape your age, your god, or your wife, I believe, but in any case haphazardly. Well, all right, I suppose you know a bit about this kind of place. Except that recently they've been closing all the bars in the country, and all the customers are like trapped rats, jumping from one sinking boat to another. And when we get down to the last bar, there will be a lot of us, old boy, we'll have to use our elbows. That moment will be the real Last Judgment. I invite you to attend, it's coming soon. You know what the regulars call this place? The Titanic. But if you look at the sign, you see the name of a mountain: Djebel Zendel. Go figure.

No, I don't want to talk about my brother today. We'll just look at all the other Musas in this dive, one by one, and imagine — as I often do — how they would have survived a shot fired in bright sunlight or how they managed never to cross paths with that writer of yours or, in a word, how they've managed not to be dead yet. There are thousands of them, believe me. They've been dragging their feet since Independence. Strolling along beaches, burying dead mothers, looking out from their balconies for hours. Damn! Sometimes this bar reminds me of the old folks' home where your Meursault put his mother: the same silence, the same discreet aging, the same end-of-life rituals. I started drinking a little early, but I've got a good excuse: my acid reflux attacks, which tend to come at night…Do you have a brother? No? Good.

Yes, I love this city, even if I adore bad-mouthing it at least as much as I do bad-mouthing women. People come here looking for money, or the sea, or a heart. No one was ever born here; everybody comes from the other side of the only mountain in sight. Incidentally, I wonder who sent you here and how you found me. It's hardly credible, you know, for years nobody believed us, Mama and me. The two of us, we ended up burying Musa, really. Yes, yes, I'll explain it to you.

Ah, there he is again…No, don't turn around. I call him "the bottle ghost." He comes here almost every day. As often as I do. We acknowledge each other without ever saying a word. I'll tell you more about him later.

III

These days, my mother's so old she looks like her own mother, or maybe her great-grandmother, or even her great-great-grandmother. Once we reach a certain age, time gives us the features of all our ancestors, combined in the soft jumble of reincarnations. And maybe, in the end, that's what the next world is, an endless corridor where all your ancestors are lined up, one after another. They turn toward the living descendant and simply wait, without words, without movements, their patient eyes fixed on a date. Mama's already living in a kind of institution, that is, in her dark little house, her little body huddled up in there like a last piece of hand luggage. The diminishment that comes with old age often strikes me as incredible, compared with the long history of a whole life. Anyway, an assembly of ancestors, condensed into a single face, seated in a circle, and facing me, as though to judge me or to ask me if I've finally found a wife. I don't know my mother's age, just as she has no idea how old I am. Before Independence, people did without exact dates; the rhythms of life were marked by births, epidemics, food shortages, et cetera. My grandmother died of typhus, an episode that served by itself to establish a calendar. My father left on a December first, I believe, and since then, that date's been a reference point for measuring the temperature of the heart, so to speak, or the beginning of the big cold.

You want the truth? I rarely go to see my mother nowadays. She lives in a house under a sky where a dead man and a lemon tree are loitering. She spends her days sweeping every corner of that house. She's rubbing out traces. Of whom, of what? Well, the traces of our secret, which was sealed one summer night, and which caused me to make the definitive leap into manhood…Be patient, I'll tell you about it. So Mama lives in a kind of village, Hadjout, formerly known as Marengo, seventy kilometers from the capital. That was where I spent the second half of my childhood and part of my youth, before going to Algiers to learn a profession (government land administration) and then returning to Hadjout to practice it. It was routine work that offered powerful nourishment to my meditations. We — my mother and I — had put as much distance as possible between us and the sound of breaking waves.

Let's take up the chronology again. We left Algiers — on that famous day when I was sure I'd spotted Zubida — and went to stay with an uncle and his family, who barely tolerated us. We lived in a hovel before being kicked out by the very people who'd taken us in. Then we lived in a little shed on the threshing floor of a colonial farm where we both had jobs, Mama as a maid of all work and me as a chore boy. The boss was this obese guy from Alsace who ended up smothered in his own fat, I believe. People said he used to torture slackers by sitting on their chests. They also said he had a protruding Adam's apple because the body of an Arab he'd swallowed was lodged in his throat. I still have memories from that period: an old priest who would sometimes bring us food, the jute sack my mother made into a kind of smock for me, the semolina dishes we'd eat on big days. I don't want to tell you about our troubles, because back then they were only a matter of hunger, not injustice. In the evening, we kids would play marbles, and if one of us didn't show up the following day, that would mean he was dead — and we'd keep on playing. It was the period of epidemics and famines. Rural life was hard, it revealed what the cities kept hidden, namely that the country was starving to death. I was afraid, especially at night, of hearing the bleak sound of men's footsteps, men who knew that Mama had no protector. Those were nights of waking and watchfulness, which I spent glued to her side. I was well and truly the *uld el-assas*, the night watchman's son and heir.

Strangely enough, we gravitated around Hadjout and its vicinity for years before we were able to settle in behind solid walls. Who knows how much cunning and patience it cost Mama to find us a house, the one she still lives in today? I sure don't. In any case, she figured out what the right move was, and I must acknowledge that she had good taste. I'll invite you to her funeral! She got herself hired as a housekeeper and waited, with me perched on her back, for Independence. The truth of the matter is that the house belonged to a family of settlers who left in a hurry, and we ended up occupying it during the first days of Independence. It's a three-room house with wallpapered walls, and in the courtyard, a dwarf lemon tree stares at the sky. There are two little sheds on the side of the house, and the entrance has a wooden doorway. I remember the vine that provided shade all along the walls and the strident peeping of the birds. Before we moved

29

into the main house, Mama and I resided in an adjacent shack, which a neighbor uses as a grocery store today. You know, I don't like to remember that period. It's as if I was pushed into begging for pity. When I was fifteen, I worked as a farm laborer. One day I got up before dawn; work was rare, and the nearest farm was three kilometers from the village. Do you know how I got a job? I'm going to confess: I let the air out of another worker's bicycle tires so I could show up earlier than he did and take his place. Yes indeed, that's hunger for you! I don't want to play the victim, but it took us years to cross the dozen or so meters that separated our hovel from the settlers' house, years of tiny, fettered steps, like slogging through mud and quicksand in a nightmare. I believe more than ten years passed before we finally got our hands on that house and declared it liberated: our property! Yes, yes, we acted like everybody else during the first days of freedom, we broke down the door, took the tableware and the candlesticks. What happened? It's a long story. I'm getting a bit lost.

The rooms in that house have always been very dark. It's like there's a wake going on all the time, the lighting's so bad. Every three months, I show up there to doze a little and look at my mother for an hour or two. After that, nothing happens. I drink some black coffee and get back on the road, go to a bar, and start waiting again. In Hadjout, everything looks pretty much the same as it did at the time when your hero accompanied his alleged mother's coffin to her grave. Nothing seems to have changed, if you don't count the new cinder-block buildings, the storefronts, and the extreme idleness that looks like it's the rule everywhere. Who, me? Nostalgic for French Algeria? No! You haven't understood a word I've said. I was just trying to tell you that back then, we Arabs gave the impression that we were waiting, not going around in circles like today. I know Hadjout and its surroundings by heart, right down to the stones in the roads. The village has grown bigger and less orderly. The cypresses have disappeared, and so have the hills, under the proliferation of unfinished houses. There are no more roads through the fields. As a matter of fact, there are no more fields.

I think it's the place where a living person can get closest to the sun without leaving the earth. According to my childhood memories, at least. But these days I don't like it anymore, that place, and I dread the day when I'll be obliged to go back there to bury Mama — who doesn't seem to want to die. At her age, passing away doesn't make sense anymore. One day, I asked myself a question that you and your people have never asked yourselves, even though it's the first clue to the puzzle. Your hero's mother — where's her grave? Yes, over in Hadjout, but where, exactly? Who's ever visited it? Who's ever located the old people's home where she lived in the book? Who's run his finger over the inscription on her gravestone? Nobody I know of. I myself have looked for that grave, but I've never found it. There were a bunch of people in the village with similar names, but the exact name of the murderer's mother is still unknown. Yes, of course, there's a possible explanation: Some of our people even decolonized the colonists' cemeteries, and you'd often see street kids playing ball with disinterred skulls, I know. That's practically become a tradition here when colonists run away. They often leave us three things: words, roads, and bones…Except that I've never found your hero's mother's grave. Did he lie about his origins? I believe so. That would explain his legendary indifference and his impossible chilliness in a country flooded with sunlight and covered with fig trees. Maybe his mother wasn't what people think she was. I know I'm just blathering here, but my suspicion is well founded. Your hero talks about that funeral in such detail, he seems to want to produce a fable, not a report. It's like a handmade reconstruction, not a private confidence. A too-perfect alibi, not a memory. Do you realize what it would mean if I could prove what I'm telling you, if I could prove your hero wasn't even present at his mother's funeral? Years later, I questioned some people from Hadjout, and guess what? Nobody remembers that name, nobody remembers a woman who died in an old folks' home or a procession of Christians in the sun. The only mother who proves this story's not an alibi is mine, and she's still at home, sweeping the courtyard around our lemon tree.

Do you want me to reveal my secret — or rather *our* secret, Mama's and mine? Here it is: One terrible night, over in Hadjout, the moon obliged me to finish the job your hero began in the sun. Anyone can blame his stars or his mother. That's a ditch I dig all the time. My god, I'm really feeling bad! I look at you and I wonder how trustworthy you are. Will you believe another version of the facts, a version previously unknown? Ah, I'm hesitating, I'm not sure. No, look, not now, we'll try another time, another day. Where to go, when you're already dead? I'm rambling. I think you want facts, not parentheses, right?

After Musa's murder, while we were still living in Algiers, my mother converted her anger into a long, spectacular mourning period that won her the sympathy of the neighbor women and a kind of legitimacy that allowed her to go out on the street, mingle with men, work in other people's houses, sell spices, and do housework without running the risk of being judged. Her femininity had died, and with it men's suspicions. I saw little of her during that time. I'd spend entire days waiting for her while she walked all over the city, conducting her investigation into Musa's death, questioning people who knew him, recognized him, or crossed his path for the last time in the course of that year, 1942. Some neighbor ladies kept me fed, and the other children in the neighborhood showed me the respect you give seriously ill or broken people. I found my status—the "dead man's brother"—almost agreeable; in fact, I didn't begin to suffer from it until I was approaching adulthood, when I learned to read and realized what an unjust fate had befallen my brother, who died in a book.

After his passing, the way my time was structured changed. I lived my life in absolute freedom, which lasted exactly forty days. The funeral didn't take place until then, you see. The neighborhood imam must have found the whole thing disturbing. Missing persons don't have funerals very often…For Musa's body was never found. As I gradually learned, my mother looked for my brother everywhere, in the morgue, at the police station in Belcourt, and she knocked on every door. To no avail. Musa had vanished, he was absolutely, perfectly, incomprehensibly dead. There had been two of them in that place of sand and salt, him and his killer, just those two. About the murderer we knew nothing. He was *el-roumi*, the foreigner, the stranger. People in the neighborhood showed my mother his picture in the newspaper, but for us he was the spitting image of all the colonists who'd grown fat on so many stolen harvests. There was nothing special about him, except for the cigarette stuck in the corner of his mouth, and his features were instantly forgettable, easy to confuse with those of all his kind. My mother visited lots of cemeteries, pestered my brother's former comrades, and tried to speak to your hero, who no longer addressed himself to anything but a scrap of newspaper found under a mat in his cell. Her efforts were in vain, but they revealed her talent for idle chatter, and her mourning period evolved into a surprising comedy, a marvelous act she put on and refined until it became a masterpiece. Virtually widowed for the second time, she turned her personal drama into a kind of business that required all who came near her to make an effort of compassion. She invented a range of illnesses in order to gather the whole tribe of female neighbors around her whenever she had so much as a migraine headache. She often pointed a finger at me as if I was an orphan, and she withdrew her affection from me very quickly, replacing it with the narrowed eyes of suspicion and the hard gaze of admonition. Oddly enough, I was treated like the dead brother and Musa like the survivor whose coffee was hot and ready at the end of the day, whose bed was made, and whose footsteps were guessed at, even coming from very far away, from downtown Algiers and the neighborhoods that were closed to us at the time. I was condemned to a secondary role because I had nothing in particular to offer. I felt guilty for being alive but also responsible for a life that wasn't my own! I was the guardian, the *assas*, like my father, watching over another body.

I also remember that weird funeral. Crowds of people; discussions lasting well into the night; us children, attracted by the lightbulbs and the many candles; and then an empty grave and a prayer for the departed. After the religious waiting period of forty days, Musa had been declared dead — swept away by the sea — and therefore the absurd service was performed, in accordance with Islam's provisions for the drowned. Then everyone left, except for my mother and me.

It's morning, I'm cold even under the blanket, I'm shivering. Musa's been dead for weeks. I hear the outside sounds — a passing bicycle, old Tawi's coughing, the squeaking of chairs, the raising of iron shutters. In my head, every voice corresponds to a woman, a time of life, a concern, a mood, or even the kind of wash that's going to be hung out that day. There's a knocking at our door. Some women have come to visit Mama. I know the script by heart: a silence, followed by sobs, then some hugs and kisses; still more tears; then one of the women lifts the curtain that divides the room in two, looks at me, smiles distractedly, and grabs the coffee jar or something else. The scene continues until sometime around noon. While it's going on, I enjoy a great deal of freedom, but it's also slightly annoying to be so invisible. Only in the afternoon, after the ritual of the scarf soaked in orange-flower water and wrapped around her head, after some interminable moaning and a long, very long silence, does Mama remember me and take me in her arms. But I know it's Musa she wants to find there, not me. And I let her do it.

My mother turned fierce, in a way. She formed some strange habits, such as very frequently washing her entire body, going to the hammam as often as possible and returning woozy and groaning. She multiplied our visits to the Sidi Abderrahman Mausoleum — we'd go on Thursdays, because Friday is the Lord's day. My memories of that place are confused: the green cloths, the enormous chandelier, the smell of incense mingled with the suffocating perfumes the women wore as they wailed and prayed, begging for a husband or fertility or love or revenge. It was a gloomy universe, neither hot nor cold, where names and portents were spoken in whispers. Try to imagine that woman: snatched away from her tribe, given in marriage to a husband who didn't know her and hastened to get away from her, the mother of two sons, one dead and one a child too silent to give her the proper cues, a woman twice widowed and forced to work for *roumis* in order to survive. She developed a taste for her martyrdom. I swear to you, when your hero dwells on his mother, I understand him better than I do when he talks about my brother. Strange, isn't it? Did I love her? Of course. Among us, the mother makes up half the world. But I've never forgiven her for the way she treated me. She seemed to resent me for a death I basically refused to undergo, and so she punished me. I don't know — I had a lot of resistance in me, and she could sense that, in a confused sort of way.

Mama knew the art of making ghosts live and, conversely, was very good at annihilating her close relatives, drowning them in the monstrous torrents of her made-up tales. She can't read, but I promise you, my friend, she would have told you the story of our family and my brother better than I can. She lied not from a desire to deceive but in order to correct reality and mitigate the absurdity that struck her world and mine. Musa's passing destroyed her, but paradoxically, it also introduced her to the macabre pleasure of a never-ending period of mourning. For a long time, not a year passed without my mother swearing she'd found Musa's body, heard his breathing or his footstep, recognized the imprints of his shoes. And for a long time, that would make me feel impossibly ashamed of her—and later, it pushed me to learn a language that could serve as a barrier between her frenzies and me. Yes, the *language*. The one I read, the one I speak today, the one that's not hers. Hers is rich, full of imagery, vitality, sudden jolts, and improvisations, but not too big on precision. Mama's grief lasted so long that she needed a new idiom to express it in. In her language, she spoke like a prophetess, recruited extemporaneous mourners, and cried out against the double outrage that consumed her life: a husband swallowed up by air, a son by water. I had to learn a language other than that one. To survive. And it was the one I'm speaking at this moment. Starting with my presumed fifteenth birthday, when we withdrew to Hadjout, I became a stern and serious scholar. Books and your hero's language gradually enabled me to name things differently and to organize the world with my own words.

Go call Musa and tell him to bring us another round. Night is falling and we have only a few more hours before the bar closes. Time is short.

I also discovered trees in Hadjout, and a sky I could almost reach. Eventually I got admitted to a school where there were a few little natives like myself. That helped me somewhat to forget Mama and her disturbing way of watching me eat and grow, as if she intended me for a sacrifice. Those were some strange years. I felt alive when I was on the street, in school, or at the farms where I worked, but going home meant stepping into a grave or at least getting a stomachache. Mama and Musa were waiting for me, each in their own fashion, and I was almost obliged to explain myself and to justify the wasted hours I'd spent not sharpening the knife of our family's vengeance. In the neighborhood, our shack was considered a sinister place. The other children called me "the widow's son." People were afraid of Mama, but they also suspected her of having committed a crime, a strange crime, otherwise why leave the city to come here and wash dishes for the *roumis*? I'm sure we must have presented a peculiar spectacle when we arrived in Hadjout: a mother hiding two carefully folded newspaper clippings in her bosom, an adolescent with his eyes on his bare feet, and some raggedy baggage. Right around that time, the murderer must have been climbing the last steps of his fame. It was the 1950s; the Frenchwomen wore short, flowered dresses, and the sun would bite their breasts.

Tell you a little about Hadjout? About the people — other than Mama — I had around me there? Well, I remember the M'rabti — just their silhouettes. In the High Plateaus, their people used to be servants, they took care of mausoleums, but then they migrated to the fertile Mitidja plain, where they picked grapes and cleaned wells. There was also the El-Mellah family—you could translate that by yourself, the "salt men"—descended from the Jews of the ancient Maghreb who were forced to preserve, in salt, the heads of those among them whom the sultan had decapitated. As for the other witnesses of my childhood, I don't remember them very well. I have fragmented memories of quarrels between neighbors, of thefts involving blankets and clothes. One of the M'rabti boys showed me how to go back home after stealing something: You had to walk backward, because that way the rural cops couldn't trace your footsteps! Family names were as vague and unstable as birth dates in those days, as I've already told you. I was the *uld el-assas*. Mama was the *armala*, the "widow": a strange, sexless status construed as perpetual mourning, where the woman is not so much a dead man's wife as the wife of death itself.

Yes, Mama's still alive today, and that fact leaves me completely indifferent. I feel bad about this, I swear, but I can't forgive her. I was her object, not her son. She doesn't speak anymore. Maybe because there's nothing left of Musa's body to carve up. I recall, time and time again, the way she would crawl inside my skin, the way she would do all the talking for me when we had visitors, her passion and her nastiness and her crazy eyes when she lost her temper.

I'll take you with me to her funeral.

The night has just turned the sky's head toward infinity. When the sun's not there to blind you, what you're looking at is God's back. Silence. I hate that word. Its multiple definitions make a lot of noise. Every time the world falls silent, the sound of raspy breathing comes back to my memory. You want another drink, or you want to leave? You should drink up while there's still time. Look, there's the bottle ghost again. I often run into him here. He's young, I think, maybe around forty. He seems intelligent, but at odds with the certitudes of his time. Yes, he comes almost every night, like me. I hold down one end of the bar, and he holds down the other end, more or less, on the side by the windows. Don't turn around, don't. If you do, he'll vanish.

IV

As I told you before, Musa's body was never found.

Consequently, my mother imposed on me a strict duty of reincarnation. For instance, as soon as I grew a little, she made me wear my dead brother's clothes, even though they were still too big for me — his undershirts, his dress shirts, his shoes — and that went on until I wore them out. I was forbidden to wander away from her, to walk by myself, to sleep in unknown places, and, while we were still in Algiers, to venture anywhere near the beach. And the sea was off-limits. Mama taught me to fear its mildest suction — so effectively that even today, when I'm walking on the shoreline where the waves die, the sensation of the sand giving way under my feet remains associated with the beginning of drowning. Deep down, Mama wanted to believe — irreversibly — that the water was the culprit, that the water had carried off her son's body. My body, therefore, became the visible *trace* of her dead son, and I ended up obeying her unspoken injunction. That's surely what explains my physical cowardice, which I of course compensated for with a restless but, to be frank, ambitionless intelligence. I was sick a lot. And throughout every illness, she'd watch over my body with a practically sinful attention, with a concern tainted by a vague undercurrent of incest. She'd reproach me for the smallest scratch as if I had wounded Musa himself. And so I was deprived of the healthy joys of youth, the awakening of the senses, and the clandestine eroticism of adolescence. I grew silent and ashamed. I avoided hammams and playing with others, and in the winter, I wore djellabas that hid me from people's eyes. It took me years to become reconciled with my body, with myself. In fact, to this day I don't know if I have. I've always kept a stiffness in my bearing, due to guilt about being alive. My arms always feel like they're asleep, I've got a glum face, I look somber and sad. Like a true night watchman's son, I sleep very little, and badly, still today — I panic at the idea of closing my eyes and falling I don't know where without my given name to anchor me. Mama transmitted her fears to me, and Musa his corpse. What could a teenager do, trapped like that between death and the mother?

I remember the rare days when I accompanied my mother as she walked the streets of Algiers in search of information about my vanished brother. She would set a brisk pace and I'd follow, my eyes fixed on her haik so I wouldn't lose her. And thus an amusing intimacy was created, the source of a brief period of tenderness. With her widow's language and her calculated whimpering, Mama collected clues and mixed genuine information with scraps left over from the previous night's dream. I can still see her with one of Musa's friends, clinging fearfully to his arm when we passed through French neighborhoods, where we counted as intruders. She'd say the names of the witnesses to the crime, citing them one by one and giving them funny nicknames, such as Sbagnioli, El-Bandi, and so forth. Remember Salamano, the dog owner your hero says was his neighbor? Mama pronounced his name

Salamandre. She cried out for revenge on "Rimon," alias Raymond, who never showed up again. He's supposed to be the origin of my brother's death, the source of that imbroglio of social mores, whores, and honor, but I wonder if he ever existed. Just as I've come to doubt the time of the killing, the presence of salt in the killer's eyes, and even, sometimes, my brother Musa's very existence.

Yes, we made an odd couple, roaming the streets of the capital like that! Much later, after the story had become a famous book and departed the country, leaving my mother and me in oblivion — even though we had suffered the loss of the book's sacrificial victim — I often went back in memory to the Belcourt neighborhood and our investigations, remembering how we'd scrutinize windows and building façades, looking for clues. When we returned home in the evening, worn out and empty-handed, we'd get funny looks from the people in the neighborhood. I think we must have been objects of compassion to some of them. One day, Mama finally got a fragile lead she could follow: Someone had given her an address. Now, Algiers was a fearful labyrinth whenever we ventured outside our perimeter, but Mama was able to find her way around. She walked without stopping, passing a cemetery and a covered market and some cafés, through a jungle of stares and cries and car horns, until she finally stopped short and gazed at a house across the street from us. It was a fine day, and I was lagging behind her, panting, because she'd been walking very fast. All along the way, I'd heard her muttering insults and threats, praying to God and her ancestors, or maybe to the ancestors of God himself, who knows. I resented her excitement a little without knowing exactly why. It was a two-story house, and the windows were closed—nothing else to report. The *roumis* in the street were eyeing us with great distrust. We remained there in silence for a long time. An hour, maybe two, and then Mama, without so much as a glance at me, crossed the street and knocked resolutely on the door. An old Frenchwoman opened it. The light behind Mama made it hard for the lady to see her, but she put her hand over her brow like a visor and examined her visitor carefully, and I watched uneasiness, incomprehension, and finally terror come over her face. She turned red, fear stood in her eyes, and she seemed about ready to scream. Then I realized Mama was reeling off the longest series of curses she'd ever pronounced. The lady at the door started to get agitated and tried to push Mama away. I was afraid for Mama, I was afraid for us. All of a sudden, the Frenchwoman collapsed unconscious on her doorstep. People had stopped to watch, I could make out their shadows behind me, little groups had formed here and there, and then someone shouted the word "Police!" A woman cried out in Arabic, telling Mama to hurry, to get away fast. That was when Mama turned around and shouted, as if she was addressing all the *roumis* in the world, "The sea will swallow you all!" Then her hand grabbed me, and we took off running like a pair of maniacs. Once we got back home, she barricaded herself behind a wall of silence. We went to bed without supper. Later she would explain to the neighbors that she'd found the house where the murderer grew up and had insulted his grandmother, maybe, and then she'd add, "Or one of his relatives, or at least a *roumi*, like him."

The murderer lived somewhere in a neighborhood not far from the sea, but many years later I discovered that he somehow had no address. There was a building with a vaguely sagging upper story above a café, poorly protected by a few trees, but its windows were always closed in those days, so I think Mama insulted an anonymous old Frenchwoman with no connection to our tragedy. Long after Independence, a new tenant opened the shutters and eliminated the last possibility of a mystery. This is all to tell you that no one was ever able to say he'd crossed the murderer's path or looked into his eyes or understood his motives. Mama questioned a great many people, so many that I eventually felt ashamed for her, as if she was begging for money and not clues. Her investigations served as a ritual to lessen her pain, and her comings and goings in the French part of the city turned, however incongruously, into opportunities to take some extended walks. I recall the day when we finally arrived at the sea, the last witness left to question. The sky was gray, and a few meters away from me was our family's immense and mighty adversary, the thief of Arabs and the killer of marauders in overalls. It was indeed the last witness on Mama's list. As soon as we got there, she pronounced Sidi Abderrahman's name and then, several times, the name of God, ordered me to stay away from the water, sat down, and massaged her aching ankles. I stood behind her, a child facing the immensity of both the crime and the horizon. Please make a note of that sentence, I think it's important. What did I feel? Nothing except the wind on my skin—it was autumn, the autumn after the murder. I tasted the salt, I saw the dense gray waves. That's all. The sea was like a wall with soft, moving edges. Far off, up in the sky, there were some heavy white clouds. I started picking up things that were lying on the sand: seashells, glass shards, bottle caps, clumps of dark seaweed. The sea told us nothing, and Mama remained motionless on the shore, like someone bending over a grave. Finally she stood up straight, looked attentively right and left, and said in a hoarse voice, "God's curse be upon you!" Then she took me by the hand and led me away from the sand, as she'd done so often before. I followed her.

So I had a ghost's childhood. There were happy moments, of course, but what did they matter, scattered through those long condolences? And I don't suppose you're putting up with this pretentious monologue of mine for the happy moments. Besides, it was you who came to me — I really wonder how you were able to track us down! You're here because you think, as I once thought, that you can find Musa or his body, identify the place where the murder was committed, and trumpet your discovery to the whole world. I understand you. You want to find a corpse, and I'm trying to get rid of one. And not just one, believe me! But Musa's body will remain a mystery. There's not a word in the book about it. That's denial of a shockingly violent kind, don't you think? As soon as the shot is fired, the murderer turns around, heading for a mystery he considers worthier of interest than the Arab's life. He continues on his way, the bedazzled martyr. As for my brother Zujj, *he's* discreetly removed from the scene and deposited I don't know where. Neither seen nor known, only killed. It's like his body was hidden by God in person! There's no trace in the official reports filed in any police station, none in the minutes of the trial, nothing in the book or in the cemeteries. Nothing. Sometimes my imagination runs even wilder than usual, I get even more lost. Maybe it was me, I'm Cain, *I* killed my brother! I've often wanted to kill Musa since he died, to get rid of his corpse, to get Mama's affection back, to recover my body and my senses, to…In any case, it's a strange story. It's your hero who does the killing, it's me who feels guilty, and I'm the one condemned to wandering…

One last memory: the visits to the hereafter, on Fridays, at the summit of Bab-el-Oued. I'm talking about El-Kettar cemetery, otherwise known as "the Perfumer" because of the former jasmine distillery located nearby. Every other Friday, we'd go to the cemetery to visit Musa's empty grave. Mama would whimper, which I found uncalled-for and ridiculous, because there wasn't anything in that hole. I remember the mint that grew in the cemetery, the trees, the winding aisles, Mama's white haik against the overly blue sky. Everybody in the neighborhood knew the hole was empty, knew Mama filled it with her prayers and an invented biography. That cemetery was the place where I awakened to life, believe me. It was where I became aware that I had a right to the fire of my presence in the world — yes, I had a right to it! — despite the absurdity of my condition, which consisted in pushing a corpse to the top of a hill before it rolled back down, endlessly. Those days, the cemetery days, were the first days when I turned to pray, not toward Mecca but toward the world. Nowadays I'm still working on better versions of those prayers. But back then I had discovered, in some obscure way, a form of sensuality. How can I explain it to you? The angle of the light, the vigorous blue of the sky, and the wind awakened me to something more disturbing than the simple satisfaction you feel after a need is met. Remember I wasn't quite ten years old, and therefore still clinging to my mother's breast. That cemetery had the attraction of a playground for me. My mother never guessed it was there that I definitively buried Musa one day, mutely shouting at him to leave me alone. Precisely *there*, in El-Kettar, an Arab cemetery. Today it's a dirty place, inhabited by fugitives and drunks. I'm told that marble is stolen from the tombs each and every night. You want to go and see it? It'll be a waste of time, you won't find anyone there, and you especially won't find a trace of that grave, which was dug like the Prophet Yusuf's well. If the body's not in it, you can't prove anything. Mama wasn't entitled to anything. Not to apologies before Independence, not to a pension afterward.

Actually, we would have had to start all over from the beginning and go a different way—the way of books, for example, and more specifically of one book, the one you bring with you every day to this bar. I read it twenty years after it came out, and it overwhelmed me with its sublime lying and its magical accord with my life. A strange story, isn't it? Let's summarize: We have a confession, written in the first person, but we have no other evidence to prove Meursault's guilt; his mother never existed, for him least of all; Musa was an Arab replaceable by a thousand others of his kind, or by a crow, even, or a reed, or whatever else; the beach has disappeared, erased by footprints or agglomerations of concrete; the only witness was a star, namely the sun; the plaintiffs were illiterate, and they moved out of town; and finally, the trial was a wicked travesty put on by idle colonials. What can you do with a man who meets you on a desert island and tells you that yesterday he killed a certain Friday? Nothing.

In this movie I saw one day, a man was mounting some long flights of stairs to reach an altar where he was supposed to have his throat cut by way of soothing some god or other. The man was climbing with his head down, moving slowly, heavily, as if exhausted, undone, subdued, but most of all as if already dispossessed of his own body. I was struck by his fatalism, by his incredible passivity. I'm sure some people thought he was defeated, but I knew he was quite simply elsewhere. I could tell from his way of carrying his own body on his own back, like a porter with a burden. Well then, I was like that man, I felt the porter's weariness more than the victim's fear.

Night has fallen. Look at this incredible city, doesn't it present a magnificent counterpoint? I think something immense, something infinite is required to balance out our human condition. I love Oran at night, despite the proliferation of rats and of all these dirty, unhealthy buildings that are constantly getting repainted; at this hour, it seems that people are entitled to something more than their routine.

Will you come tomorrow?

V

I admire your patience, cunning pilgrim that you are—
I think I'm really starting to like you! For once, I have
a chance to talk about this story...Picture an old whore
dazed by an excess of men; she and this story of mine
share some features. It's like a text written on parchment
and scattered all over the world; it's brittle, patched up,
no longer recognizable, infinitely rehashed—and yet
look at you, sitting beside me and hoping for something
new, something never heard before. This story doesn't
suit your quest for purity, I swear to you. If you want
to light your way, you should look for a woman, not
a dead man.

Shall we order the same wine as yesterday? I love its
rough edges, its freshness. The other day, a wine pro-
ducer was telling me his troubles. It's impossible to find
workers, because the activity is considered *haram*, illicit.
Even the country's banks are piling on and refusing him
credit! Ha, ha! I've always wondered, what's the reason
for this complicated relationship with wine? Why is it
treated as though it's of the devil, when it's supposed to
be flowing profusely in Paradise? Why is it forbidden
down here and promised up there? Drunken driving.
Maybe God doesn't want humanity to drink while it's
driving the universe to its place, holding on to the steering wheel of heaven...Yes, yes, I agree, the argument's

a bit muddled. As you're starting to realize, I like to ramble.

You're here to find a corpse and write your book. But you should be aware that even though I know the story—all too well—I know virtually nothing about its geography. Algiers is only a shadow in my mind. I almost never go there. Sometimes I see it on television, looking like an outdated actress left over from the days of revolutionary theater. So there's no geography in this story. Generally speaking, it takes place in three settings of national importance: the city, whether that one or another one; the mountains, where you take refuge when you're attacked or you want to make war; and the village, which is for each and every one of us the ancestral home. Everybody wants a village wife and a big-city whore. Just by looking out the windows of this bar, I can sort the local humans for you according to one of those three addresses. And so when Musa went away into the mountains to speak to God about eternity, Mama and I left the city and went back to the village. That's all. There was nothing more until I learned to read and the little scrap of newspaper Mama kept between her breasts for so long—the one that reported the murder of Musa/Zujj—suddenly became a book with a name. Just think, we're talking about one of the most-read books in the world. My brother might have been famous if your author had merely deigned to give him a name. H'med or Kaddour or Hammou, just a name, damn it! Mama could have had a martyr's widow's pension, and I could have had a known, recognized brother, a brother I could have prided myself on. But no, he didn't name him, because if he had, my brother would have caused the murderer a problem with his conscience: You can't easily kill a man when he has a given name.

Let's go back. It's always a good thing to go back and review the basics. A Frenchman kills an Arab who's lying on a deserted beach. It's two o'clock in the afternoon on a summer day in 1942. Five gunshots, followed by a trial. The killer's condemned to death for having buried his mother badly and spoken of her with too much indifference. Technically, the killing itself is due either to the sun or to pure idleness. A pimp named Raymond is angry with a whore and asks your hero to write her a threatening letter, which he does. Things go downhill, and then the story seems to resolve itself in a murder. The Arab is killed because the murderer thinks he wants to avenge the prostitute, or maybe because he has the insolence to take a siesta. You find my summary of your book unsettling, eh? But it's the naked truth. All the rest is nothing but embellishments, the products of your writer's genius. Afterward, nobody bothers about the Arab, his family, or his people. When the murderer leaves prison, he writes a book that becomes famous, in which he recounts how he stood up to God, a priest, and the absurd. You can turn that story in all directions, it doesn't hold up. It's the story of a crime, but the Arab isn't even killed in it — well, he *is* killed, but barely, delicately, with the fingertips, as it were. He's the second most important character in the book, but he has no name, no face, no words. Does that make any sense to you, educated man that you are? The story's absurd! It's a blatant lie. Have another glass, it's on me. Your Meursault doesn't describe a world in his book, he describes the end of a world. A world where property is useless, marriage practically unnecessary, and weddings halfhearted, where it's as though people are already sitting on their luggage, empty, superficial, holding on to their sick and fetid dogs, incapable of forming more than two sentences or pronouncing four words in a row. Robots! Yes, that's the word, it wasn't coming to me. I remember that little woman, a Frenchwoman, the one the writer-killer describes so well. He observes her one day in a restaurant. Jerky movements, shining eyes, tics, anxiety about the bill, robot gestures. I also remember the pendulum clock that was right in the middle of Hadjout, and I think it's that Frenchwoman's twin. The thing stopped for good a few years before Independence, it seems to me.

So the mystery struck me as more and more unfathomable. See, I've got a mother and a murder on *my* back too. Me too. It's fate. I too have killed, in accordance with the desires of this earth, one day when I had nothing to do. Ah! I swore to myself so many times I'd never revisit that episode, but every move I make either dramatizes it or evokes it involuntarily. I was waiting for a little nosynose like yourself to come along, someone I could finally tell this tale to...

Inside my head, the map of the world is a triangle. At the top, in Bab-el-Oued, there's the house where Musa was born. Lower down, overlooking the Algiers coast, there's the place with no address where the murderer never came into the world. And finally, even lower, there's the beach. The beach, yes indeed! These days it doesn't exist anymore, or it's slowly shifted itself elsewhere. According to witnesses, there was a time when you could still spot the little wooden bungalow at the far end of the beach. The back of the house rested against the rocks, and the pilings that held it up in front went straight down into the water. The commonness of the place struck me when I went there with Mama that autumn, the autumn after the crime. I've already described that scene to you, right? Me and Mama on the seashore, me ordered to stay back, and Mama facing the waves and cursing them? I have that feeling every time I get close to the sea. A bit of terror at first, an accelerated heartbeat, followed rather quickly by disappointment. It was as if the place was simply too confined! It seemed like trying to squeeze the *Iliad* into a narrow space on the street, between a grocery store and a barber shop. Yes, the scene of the crime was in fact a terrible letdown. In my view, my brother Musa's story needs the entire earth! Ever since that day, I've cultivated a wild hypothesis: Musa wasn't killed on that famous Algiers beach! There must be another, hidden place, a setting that was disappeared. That would explain everything, all at once! Why the murderer was so relaxed after being sentenced to death and even after his execution, why my brother was never found, and why the court preferred judging a man who didn't weep over his mother's death to judging a man who killed an Arab.

I sometimes thought about poking around that beach at the exact hour of the crime. That is, during the summer, when the sun's so close to earth it can make you crazy or drive you to shed blood, but that would be a futile exercise. Besides, the sea bothers me. I'm definitively afraid of the water. I don't like to go swimming—the waves swallow me up too fast. *"Malou khouya, malou majache.*

El b'har eddah âliyah rah ou ma wellache." (Where is he, my brother, why didn't he come back? The sea took him from me, he never came back.) I love that old song. It's a local tune. A man sings about his brother, who was swept out to sea. I've got several images in my head, but I think I've been drinking a bit too fast. The truth is, I've actually done it. Six times...Yes, I went there six times, there to that beach. But I never found anything, no empty cartridges, no footsteps, no witnesses, no dried blood on the rock. Nothing. I looked for years. Until one Friday, ten years ago, more or less, the day when I *saw* him. Under a rock, a few meters from the water, I suddenly saw a silhouette that merged with a dark wedge of shadow. I'd walked on the beach for a long time, as I recall. I intended to get knocked out by the sun, to suffer sunstroke or a fainting spell and thus relive to some degree what your author describes. And I admit it, I'd also had a lot to drink. The sun was overwhelming, like a heavenly accusation. It shattered into needles on the sand and on the sea but never ever flagged. At one point, I had the impression of knowing where I was going, but that impression was surely mistaken. And then, down at the end of the beach, I spotted a tiny spring flowing in a trickle over the sand behind the rock. And I saw *a man*, dressed in overalls and nonchalantly lying there. I looked at him with fear and fascination; he seemed to barely notice me. One of us two was an insistent ghost, and the shadow — very deep, very black — had the coolness of a threshold. Then...then it seemed that the scene veered off into some sort of amusing delirium. When I raised my hand, the shadow did the same. And when I took a step to the side, it turned and changed its resting point. Then I stopped, with my heart pounding, and I realized I had my mouth hanging open, like an idiot, and no weapon, not even a knife. I was sweating profusely, the big drops burning my eyes. No one was around, and the sea was mute. I knew for sure I was looking at a reflection, but I had no idea of what! I groaned out loud, and the shadow flickered. I took a backward step, and the shadow did the same, in a kind of weird contraction. I found myself stretched out on my back, shivering with cold, bludgeoned by bad wine. I'd walked backward about ten meters before collapsing in tears. Yes, I assure you, I wept for Musa years after his death. My efforts to reconstruct the crime at the scene where it had been committed were leading me to an impasse, to a ghost, to madness. All of which is to tell you there's no point in your going to the cemetery, or to Bab-el-Oued, or to the beach. You won't find anything. I've already tried, my friend. I told you right from the start: This story takes place somewhere in someone's head, in mine and in yours and in the heads of people like you. In a sort of beyond.

Don't do any geographical searching — that's the point I'm trying to make.

You'll get a better grasp on my version of the facts if you accept the idea that this story is like an origin myth: Cain comes here to build cities and roads, and to domesticate people and soil and plants. Zujj is the poor relative, loafing in the sunshine, his whole attitude so lazy it's evident he owns nothing, not even a flock of sheep, that could arouse envy or motivate murder. In a certain way, *your* Cain killed *my* brother for...nothing! Not even for his livestock.

We should stop here. You've got enough material to write a good book, no? The story of the Arab's brother. Another Arab story. You're hooked…

Ah, the ghost, my double…see him there, behind you, holding his beer? I've been taking note of his maneuvers. He's getting progressively closer to us, ever so casually. A real crab, that one. The ritual is always the same. He spreads out his newspaper and reads it diligently during the first hour. Then he cuts out articles and news items — relating to murders, I think, because I once took a look at what he'd left on the table. Next he looks out the window and drinks. Then the contours of his silhouette get blurry and he himself becomes diaphanous and almost fades away. Like a reflection. You forget he's there, you hardly step around him when the bar's crowded. No one's ever heard him speak. The waiter seems to guess what he wants to order. He's always wearing that same old jacket, worn at the elbows, and the same bangs on his big forehead, and his look is always the same, intelligent and cold. And let's not forget the cigarette. His eternal cigarette, connecting him to heaven by the fine coil of smoke twisting and rising above him. He's hardly ever looked at me, despite the years we've been neighbors in here. Ha, ha, I'm his Arab. Or maybe he's mine.

Good night, my friend.

VI

I used to love stealing the bread Mama hid on top of the armoire and then watching her look all over for it, muttering curses the whole time. One night a few months after Musa's death, when we were still living in Algiers, I waited until she fell asleep, swiped the key to the trunk where she kept supplies, and ate almost all the sugar. The next morning she panicked, she was grumbling to herself, and then she started scratching her face with her fingernails and wailing about her plight: a husband vanished, a son killed, and another son observing her with an almost cruel joy in his eyes. Well, yes! I remember that, I remember feeling a strange jubilation at seeing her really suffering for once. To prove my existence, I had to disappoint her. It was like fate. That tie bound us together, deeper than death.

One day Mama wanted me to go to the neighborhood mosque, which served more or less as a day-care center, supervised by a young imam. It was summer, and the sun was so harsh Mama had to drag me into the street by my hair. I struggled like a maniac and managed to get free of her. Then I shouted an insult and, still holding the bunch of grapes she'd tried to coax me with just a minute or two before, I ran away. I ran until I tripped and fell and the grapes got completely crushed in the dust. I cried my eyes out and ended up going to the mosque, all contrite. I don't know what came over me, but when the imam asked what was causing me such grief, I accused another kid of hitting me. I think that was my first lie. My own personal version of eating the forbidden fruit. Because from then on, I became wily and deceitful, I started to grow up. Now, that first lie of mine, I told it on a summer day. Just like your hero the murderer—bored, solitary, examining his own tracks, spinning his wheels, trying to make sense of the world by trampling the bodies of Arabs.

Arab. I never felt Arab, you know. Arab-ness is like Negro-ness, which only exists in the white man's eyes. In our neighborhood, in our world, we were Muslims, we had given names, faces, and habits. Period. The others were "the strangers," the *roumis* God brought here to put us to the test, but whose days were numbered anyway: One day or another, they would leave, there was no doubt about that. And so nobody responded to them, people clammed up in their presence, leaned on the wall, and waited. Your writer-murderer was wrong, my brother and his friend had no intention whatsoever of killing them, him and his pimp friend. They were just waiting for them to leave, all of them, your hero, the pimp, and the thousands and thousands of others. We all knew it, we knew it from early childhood, we didn't even need to talk about it: We knew one day they'd eventually leave. When we happened to pass through a European neighborhood, we used to amuse ourselves by pointing at the houses and divvying them up like spoils of war. One of us would say, "This one's mine, I touched it first!" and set off a frenzy of claims and counterclaims. We were five years old when we started doing that, can you imagine?

As if our intuition was telling us what would happen when Independence came, but leaving out the weapons.

And so my brother had to be seen through your hero's eyes in order to become an "Arab" and consequently die. On that miserable morning in the summer of 1942 — as I've already mentioned several times — Musa had announced that he'd be home earlier than usual. Which annoyed me a little, because it meant I'd have less time for playing in the street. Musa was wearing his blue overalls and his espadrilles. He drank his café au lait, looked at the walls the way people today browse through their phones, and then suddenly stood up, maybe after coming to a definitive decision about his schedule and the hour of his rendezvous with some friends. Every day, or almost, went the same way: a foray in the morning, followed — if there was no work at the port or in the market — by long hours of idleness. Musa slammed the door behind him, leaving my mother's question unanswered: "Will you bring home some bread?"

One point in particular keeps nagging at me: How did my brother end up on that beach? We'll never know. That detail's an immeasurable mystery. You can get dizzy thinking about it and then wondering how a man could lose his name, plus his life, plus his own corpse, all in a single day. Yes, that's it, basically. This story — I'm going to allow myself to get a little bombastic here — it's everybody's story these days. He was Musa to us, his family, his neighbors, but it was enough for him to venture a few meters into the French part of the city, a single glance from one of them was enough, to make him lose everything, starting with his name, which went floating off into some blind spot in the landscape. In fact, Musa didn't do anything that day but get too close to the sun, in a way. He was supposed to meet one of his friends, a certain Larbi, who as I recall played the flute. Incidentally, he's never been found, this Larbi guy. He vanished from the neighborhood to avoid my mother, the police, the whole story, and even the story in your book. All that's left of him is his first name, which makes an odd echo: Larbi l'Arabe, Larbi the Arab. But he's a false twin, he couldn't be more anonymous... Oh, right, there's still the prostitute! I never talk about her, because her part is truly insulting. It's a tall tale invented by your hero. Did he have to make up such an improbable story, a working whore whose brother wanted to avenge her? I acknowledge that your hero had the talent to create a tragedy out of a newspaper clipping and bring a mad emperor to life out of a fire, but I confess, he disappointed me there. Why a whore? To insult Musa's memory, to smear him and thus diminish the gravity of the author's own misdeed? I've come to doubt that. I think rather that his twisted mind conceived some abstract characters. This country, our land, in the form of two imaginary women: the famous Marie, brought up in a greenhouse of impossible innocence, and the alleged sister of Musa alias Zujj, a distant symbol of our land, plowed by customers and passersby, reduced to dependence on an immoral, violent pimp. A whore whose honor her Arab brother feels himself dutybound to avenge. If you had met me a few decades ago, I would have served you up the version with the prostitute slash Algerian land and the settler who abuses her with repeated rapes and violence. But I've gained some distance now. We never had a sister, my brother Zujj and I, period.

I can't help wondering, over and over, what was Musa doing on that beach that day? I don't know. Idleness is an easy explanation, and blaming it on destiny is too pompous. Maybe the proper question, after all, is the following: What was *your* hero doing on that beach? And not only that day but every day, going a long way back! A century, to be frank. No, believe me, I'm not one of those. It doesn't matter that he was French and I'm Algerian, except that Musa was on the beach first, and it was your hero who came looking for him. Reread the paragraph in the book. He himself admits he was slightly lost when they came upon the two Arabs, almost by chance. What I mean to say is, your hero had a life that shouldn't have led him to such murderous idleness. He was starting to get famous, he was young and free, he had a paying job, and he was capable of seeing things as they are. He should have moved to Paris by then, or married Marie. Why did he go to that very beach on that very day? What's inexplicable is not only the murder but also the fellow's life. He's a corpse that magnificently describes the quality of the light in this country while stuck in some hereafter with no gods and no hells. Nothing but blinding routine. His life? If he hadn't killed and written, nobody would have remembered him.

I want some more to drink. Call him.

Hey, Musa!

It was already the case some years ago, and it's still the case today: When I add things up and go over my lists, I'm always a little surprised. In the first place, the beach doesn't really exist, and also there's Musa's alleged sister, who's either an allegory or just a pathetic last-minute excuse. And then there are the witnesses: One by one, they turn out to be pseudonyms, or not really neighbors, or memories, or people who fled after the crime. My list is down to two couples and an orphan. On one side, your Meursault and his mother; on the other, Mama and Musa; and right in the middle, unable to be the son of either, me, sitting in this bar and trying to hold your attention.

Judging from your enthusiasm, the book's success is still undiminished, but I repeat, I think it's an awful swindle. After Independence, the more I read of your hero's work, the more I had the feeling I was pressing my face against the window of a big room where a party was going on that neither my mother nor I had been invited to. Everything happened without us. There's not a trace of our loss or of what became of us afterward. Not a single trace, my friend! The whole world eternally witnesses the same murder in the blazing sun, but no one saw anything, and no one watched us recede into the distance. No one! There's good reason to get a little angry, don't you think? If only your hero had been content with bragging, without going so far as to write a book! There were thousands like him back then, but it was his talent that made his crime perfect.

Say, the ghost is absent again this evening. Two nights in a row. He must be conducting the dead, or reading books nobody understands.

VII

No, thanks, no café au lait for me! I despise that concoction.

Actually, it's Fridays I don't like. I often spend them on the balcony of my apartment, looking at the people, the streets, and the mosque. It's so imposing, it's as though it prevents you from seeing God. I've lived there — I'm on the fourth floor — for twenty years now, I think. The whole place is falling into ruin. When I lean over my balcony and observe young children playing, it seems like I'm watching a live broadcast of the new generations, in ever-increasing numbers, as they push the old ones toward the edge of the cliff. It's shameful, but I feel hatred when I see them. They're stealing something from me. I slept very badly last night.

My neighbor's an invisible man who takes it upon himself, every weekend, to read the Koran at the top of his voice all night long. Nobody dares tell him to stop, because it's God who's making him shout. I myself don't dare, I'm marginal enough in this city as it is. His voice is nasal, plaintive, and obsequious. It sounds as if he's alternating roles, from torturer to victim and back. I always react that way when I hear someone recite the Koran. I get the feeling it's not a book, it's a dispute between a heaven and a creature! As far as I'm concerned, religion is public transportation I never use. This God — I like traveling in his direction, on foot if necessary, but I don't want to take an organized trip. I've loathed Fridays ever since Independence, I think. Am I a believer? I've dealt with the heaven question by recognizing the obvious: I realized very young that among all those who nattered on about my condition, whether angels, gods, devils, or books, I was the only one who knew the sorrow and obligation of death, work, and sickness. I alone pay the electric bill, I alone will be eaten by worms in the end. So get lost! And therefore I detest religions and submission. Who wants to run panting after a father who has never set foot on earth, has never had to know hunger or work for a living?

My father? Oh, I've told you everything I know about him. I learned to write his name in my school notebooks, the way you write an address. A family name and nothing else. There's no other trace of him; I don't even have an old jacket or a photograph. Mama always refused to describe his looks or his character, to give him a body or share the smallest memory with me. And I had no paternal uncles and no tribe to help reestablish his outline. Nothing. And so, when I was a little boy, I imagined him as rather like Musa, but bigger. Immense, gigantic, capable of fits of cosmic anger, sitting at the world's border, doing his night watchman's job. My theory is, it was either weariness or cowardice that caused him to leave. You know, maybe I've taken after him. I left my own family before I had one, for I've never been married. Sure, I've known the love of lots of women, but it never untied the heavy, suffocating knot of secrets that bound me to my mother. After all these years of bachelorhood, here's my conclusion: I have always nurtured a mighty distrust of women. Basically, I've never believed them.

Mother, death, love — everyone shares, unequally, those three poles of fascination. The truth is that women have never been able to free me from my own mother, from the smoldering anger I felt toward her, or to protect me from her eyes, which followed me everywhere for a long time. In silence. As if they were asking me why I hadn't found Musa's body or why I'd survived instead of him or why I'd come into the world. And then you have to consider the modesty that was obligatory in those days. Accessible women were rare, and in a village like Hadjout, you couldn't come across a woman with her face uncovered, much less talk to one. I didn't have any female cousin anywhere around. The only part of my life that was anything like a love story was what I had with Meriem. She's the only woman who found the patience to love me and lead me back to life. It wasn't quite summer yet when I met her, in 1963. Everyone was riding the wave of post-Independence enthusiasm, and I can still remember her wild hair and her passionate eyes, which come and visit me sometimes in insistent dreams. After my relationship with Meriem, I became aware that women would get themselves out of my way, they'd make, so to speak, a detour, as if they could instinctively tell I was another woman's son and not a potential companion. My appearance didn't help much either. I'm not talking about my body, I'm talking about what a woman divines or desires in a man. Women have an intuition about what's unfinished and avoid men who cling to their youthful doubts too long. Meriem was the only one willing to defy my mother, even though she almost never met her and didn't really know her except from running up against my silences and my hesitations. She and I saw each other about ten times that summer. Then we had a correspondence that lasted several months, and then she stopped writing to me and everything dissolved. Maybe because of a death or a marriage or a change of address. Who knows? There's an old mailman in my neighborhood who wound up in prison because he'd fallen into the habit of throwing away his undelivered letters at the end of each day.

Today's Friday. It's the day closest to death in my calendar. People dress ridiculously, they stroll through the streets at noon still wearing pajamas, practically, shuffling around in slippers as though Friday exempts them from the demands of civility. In our country, religious faith encourages laziness in private matters and authorizes spectacular negligence every Friday. You'd think men observed God's day by being completely scruffy and slovenly. Have you noticed that people are dressing worse and worse? Without care, without elegance, without concern for the harmony of colors or nuances. Nothing. Old men like me, fond of red turbans, vests, bow ties, or beautiful, shiny shoes, are becoming rarer and rarer. We seem to be disappearing at the same rate as the public parks. It's the Friday prayer hour I detest the most — and always have, ever since childhood, but even more for the past several years. The imam's voice, shouting through the loudspeakers, the rolled-up prayer rugs tucked under people's arms, the thundering minarets, the garish architecture of the mosque, and the hypocritical haste of the devout on their way to water and bad faith, ablutions and recitations. You'll see this spectacle everywhere on Friday, my friend — you're not in Paris anymore. It's almost always the same scene and has been for years. The neighbors start to stir, dragging their feet and moving slow, a long time after their pack of kids, who wake up early and swarm around, like maggots on my body. The new car gets washed and rewashed. Then there's the sun, which runs its course uselessly on that eternal day, and the almost physical sensation of the idleness of the whole cosmos, reduced to balls that must be washed and verses that must be recited. Sometimes I get to thinking: Now that these people don't have to go underground and the land is theirs, they don't know where to go. Friday? It's not a day when God rested, it's a day when he decided to run away and never come back. I know this from the hollow sound that persists after the men's prayer, and from their faces pressed against the window of supplication. And from their coloring, the complexion of people who respond to fear of the absurd with zeal. As for me, I don't like anything that rises to heaven, I only like things affected by gravity. I'll go so far as to say I abhor religions. All of them! Because they falsify the weight of the world. Sometimes I feel like busting through the wall that separates me from my neighbor, grabbing him by the throat, and yelling at him to quit reciting his sniveling prayers, accept the world, open his eyes to his own strength, his own dignity, and stop running after a father who has absconded to heaven and is never coming back. Have a look at that group passing by, over there. Notice the little girl with the veil on her head, even though she's not old enough to know what a body is, or what desire is. What can you do with such people? Eh?

On Friday all the bars are closed and I have nothing to do. People look at me strangely, because despite my age I entreat no one and reach out to no one. It doesn't seem right to be so close to death without feeling close to God. "Forgive them [my God], for they know not what they do." With my whole body and all my hands, I'm clinging to this life, which I alone shall lose and which I'm the sole witness to. As for death, I got close to it years ago, and it never brought me closer to God. It only made me long to have more powerful, more voracious senses and increased the depth of my own mystery. The others are marching to death in single file, and me, I've come back from it, and I can report there's nothing on the other side but an empty beach in the sun. What would I do if I had an appointment with God and on the way I met a man who needed help fixing his car? I don't know. I'm the fellow whose vehicle broke down, not the driver looking for the way to sainthood. Of course, I keep quiet here in the city, and my neighbors don't like my independence, though they envy it and would be happy to make me pay for it. Children fall silent when I approach them, except for some who mutter insults as I go by, but they're always ready to run away if I turn around, the little cowards. Centuries ago, I might have been burned alive for my convictions, and for the empty red wine bottles found in the neighborhood Dumpsters. Nowadays, people just avoid me. I feel something close to divine pity for this teeming anthill and its disorganized hopes. How can you believe God has spoken to only one man, and that one man has stopped talking forever? Sometimes I page through their book, *the* Book, and what I find there are strange redundancies, repetitions, lamentations, threats, and daydreams. I get the impression that I'm listening to a soliloquy spoken by some old night watchman, some *assas*.

Ah, Fridays!

Remember the bar ghost, the guy who has a way of circling around us, as though he's trying to hear me better or steal my story? Well, I often wonder what he does with his Fridays. Does he go to the beach? To the movies? Does he too have a mother, or a wife he likes to kiss? Intriguing mystery, eh? Have you noticed that generally, on Fridays, the sky looks like sagging sails, the shops close, and the whole universe is deserted by noon? That's when a kind of feeling grips my heart, the sense that I must have committed some secret fault. I went through so many awful days like that in Hadjout, and always with the sensation of being stuck forever in a deserted railroad station.

For decades I've stood on my balcony and observed these people: killing one another, rising again, waiting forever, hesitating over their departure schedules, shaking their heads, talking to themselves, digging in their pockets like panicked travelers, looking at the sky instead of a watch, surrendering to strange venerations, digging holes to lie in so they can meet their God sooner. I've observed these people so often that today I see them as a single person, a man I avoid talking to for any length of time and keep at a respectful distance. My balcony overlooks the city's public space: broken playground slides, a few scrawny, tormented trees, some dirty staircases, some windblown plastic bags clinging to people's legs, other balconies decorated with unidentified laundry, water cisterns, and satellite dishes. My neighbors bustle about before my eyes like familiar miniatures: a mustachioed retired military man who washes his car with infinitely drawn-out, almost masturbatory pleasure; another man, sad-eyed and very dark, who's discreetly charged with handling the rental of chairs, tables, dishes, lightbulbs, and so forth for funerals as well as for marriages. There's a fireman with a bad limp who regularly beats his wife and who stands on the landing of their apartment at dawn—because she always ends up throwing him out—and begs her forgiveness, all the while shouting his own mother's name. And nothing else but that, for God's sake! Well, I suppose you're familiar with that sort of thing, even though you've lived in exile for years, or so you claim.

I'm telling you about this because it's one side of my universe. My other balcony, the invisible one in my head, looks out over the scene with the white-hot beach, the impossible trace of Musa's body, and the sun, fixed above the head of a man holding a cigarette or a revolver, I can't really tell. I see this scene from far off. The man has brown skin, he's wearing a pair of shorts a bit too long for him, and his silhouette's rather slight; he seems to be propelled, his very muscles seem to be tensed, by some blind force, as if he's a robot. In one corner, there are a few pilings holding up a bungalow, and at the other end, the rock that marks the limit of this universe. The scene never changes, and I beat against it like a fly against a windowpane. It's impossible to penetrate. I can't step inside and run across the sand and change the order of things. What do I feel when I see this scene, over and over? The same things I felt when I was seven years old. Curiosity, excitement, the wish to pass through the screen or follow the white rabbit. Sadness, because I can't clearly make out Musa's face. Also anger. And always, the urge to weep. Feelings grow old slowly, not as fast as skin. Maybe someone who dies at the age of a hundred doesn't feel anything more than the fear that grips us when we're six and it's nighttime and our mother comes in to turn out the light.

In this scene where nothing moves, your hero doesn't look at all like the other one, the one I killed. He was big, vaguely blond, with enormous circles under his eyes, and he always wore the same checked shirt. Who was he, this other one? You're wondering, right? There's always another, my friend. In love, in friendship, or even on a train, there he is, the other, sitting across from you and staring at you, or turning his back to you and deepening the perspectives of your solitude.

And so there's one in my story too.

VIII

I squeezed the trigger and fired twice. Two bullets. One in the belly, and the other in the neck. That makes seven all told, I thought at once, absurdly. (But the first five, the ones that killed Musa, had been fired twenty years earlier...)

Mama was behind me, and I could feel her eyes on my back like a hand pushing me, holding me upright, guiding my arm, slightly tilting my head at the moment when I took aim. The face of the man I'd just killed kept its look of surprise—big, round eyes and grotesquely contorted mouth. A dog barked in the distance. The lemon tree in the courtyard of our house trembled under the black, hot sky. My body was entirely rigid, as though frozen by a cramp. The butt of the gun was sticky with perspiration. It was night, but everything was clearly visible. Because of the luminous moon. It looked so close, you could have jumped up and touched it. The man was giving off his last drops of terror sweat. He's going to sweat until he returns all his water to the earth, I said to myself, and then he'll steep for a while and mingle with the mud. I began to imagine his death as a disintegration of elements. The monstrousness of my crime would vanish with them somehow. It was not a murder but a *restitution*. I also thought—even if it may seem odd for a kid like me—that he wasn't a Muslim, and that therefore his death wasn't forbidden. But that was a coward's thought, and I knew it right away. I remember the look in his eyes. He wasn't even accusing me, I don't think, he was just staring at me the way you stare at an unexpected dead end. Mama was still behind me, and I could gauge her relief by her breathing, which calmed down and suddenly became very soft. Before, she'd done nothing but wheeze. ("Ever since Musa died," a voice said to me.) The moon was looking on too, it too; the whole sky seemed to be nothing but moon. It had already begun to soothe the earth, and the damp heat was rapidly diminishing. The dog somewhere on the dark horizon started barking a second time, at length, and nearly roused me from the languor I'd fallen into. I found it ridiculous that a man could die so easily, that he could conclude our acquaintance with such a theatrical, almost comic collapse. My temples were throbbing from the deafening panic in my heart.

Mama made no move, but I knew she had just withdrawn her immense vigilance from the universe. She was packing her bags, on her way to meet her old age, which she'd finally earned. I knew it instinctively. I could feel the icy flesh in my right armpit, under the arm that had just destroyed the balance of things. "Maybe things are finally going to return to the way they were," someone said. I heard voices inside my head. Maybe it was Musa who was talking. When you kill someone, there's a part of you that immediately starts devising an explanation, making up an alibi, putting together a version of the facts that washes your hands clean, even though they still smell of gunpowder and sweat. But I didn't really think I had anything to worry about. I'd known for years that when I killed somebody, I wouldn't have to be saved, judged, or questioned by anyone. Nobody kills a specific individual during a war. It's not a question of murder, it's a question of battle, of combat. Now, outside, far from both the beach and our house, there was indeed a war going on, the War of Liberation, which stifled rumors of all other crimes. It was the first days of Independence, and the French were running in all directions, stuck between the sea and defeat, and the people, your people, were jubilant, they arose, dressed in their overalls, they extricated themselves from their siestas under the rocks and started killing in their turn. That would suffice as my alibi, just in case—but I knew, in the deepest part of me, that I wouldn't need any such thing. My mother would see to that. And besides, he was only a Frenchman, no doubt running away from his own conscience. Basically I felt relieved, unburdened, free in my own body, which had finally stopped being destined to murder. Like a flash—like a shot!—I had a sense of immense space, I grew dizzy at the possibility of my own freedom, I felt the hot, sensuous dampness of the earth and smelled the lemony perfume in the hot air. It occurred to me that I could finally take in a movie or go swimming with a woman.

The whole night abruptly gave way and turned into a sigh—like after sex, I swear. I even came close to groaning, I remember that distinctly, because of the odd shame I still feel whenever I think back on that moment. We remained like that a good while, each of us busy examining his or her eternity. The Frenchman who'd had the bad luck to seek refuge in our house on that summer night in

1962; me, still holding my arm out long after the murder; and Mama, with her monstrous demand finally satisfied. And all of us behind the world's back, during the cease-fire of July 1962.

On that hot night, nothing had suggested that a murder was about to happen. You're asking me what I felt afterward? Huge relief. A kind of worthiness, but without honor. Something deep inside me sat down, curled up into a ball, took its head in its hands, and sighed so profoundly that I was touched and tears sprang to my eyes. Then I raised them and looked around me. Again I was surprised by the extent of the courtyard where I had just executed an unknown person. It was as if perspectives were opening up and I could finally breathe. Whereas I'd always lived like a prisoner until then, confined within the perimeter established by Musa's death and my mother's vigilance, I now saw myself standing upright, at the heart of a vast territory: the whole nocturnal earth, the gift of that night. When my heart regained its place, all other objects did the same.

Mama, for her part, was scrutinizing the Frenchman's body, already measuring him in her head for the grave we were going to dig. What she said to me got lost inside my skull, but then she repeated herself, and this time I understood her words: "Work fast!" She spoke in the sharp, firm tone you use when ordering someone to do chores. There was not only a corpse to be buried, there was also a scene to be cleared and cleaned up, like a stage in a theater after the last act is over. (Sweep away the beach sand, stash the body in a fold of the horizon, push away the two Arabs' famous rock and chuck it behind the hill, make the weapon dissolve like foam, flip the switch to light up the sky again and restart the panting of the sea, and, finally, head for the bungalow to meet up with the frozen characters of this story.) Oh, yes, one last detail. I had to take hold of the clock that registers all the hours of my life and turn the hands back until they showed the exact time when Musa was murdered: *Zujj*, two o'clock in the afternoon. I could hear the works clicking as they resumed their clear, regular ticktock. Because just imagine, I killed the Frenchman around two in the morning. And from that moment on, Mama began to grow old naturally, she was no longer preserved by spite, wrinkles folded her face into a thousand pages, and her own ancestors at last seemed calm and capable of approaching her to open the lengthy debate that leads to the end.

As for me, what shall I tell you? Life had been given back to me at last, even if I had a new cadaver to drag around. At least, I told myself, it's not mine anymore, it's an unknown person's. Our weird family, composed of the dead and the disinterred, kept that night a secret. We buried the *roumi*'s body in a patch of ground near the courtyard. Ever since, Mama's been watching for a possible resurrection. We did our digging by moonlight. Nobody seemed to have heard the two shots. As I've told you, there was a lot of killing going on back then, during the first days of Independence. It was a strange period, when you could kill without worrying about it; the war was over, but deaths were disguised as accidents or the result of ongoing feuds. Besides, a Frenchman who disappeared in the village? Nobody spoke of that. At least, not in the beginning.

There you are, now you know our family secret. You and the treacherous ghost behind you. I've watched his progress — he gets closer and closer to us from one evening to the next. Maybe he heard everything I said, but I don't care.

No, I never really knew that man, the Frenchman I killed. He was big, and I remember his checked shirt, his camouflage jacket, and his smell. That was what first revealed his presence to me that night, when I woke with a start and went outside to identify the source of the noise, which had awakened Mama too. The muffled noise of a fall, followed by an even noisier silence and a dirty smell of fear. He was so white that his skin proved a disadvantage to him in the darkness where he was hiding.

As I've told you, the night was transparent, like a sheer curtain. And I've also told you there was a lot of random killing back then. The French OAS did some of it, and so did the FLN *djounoud* who joined up at the eleventh hour. Those were troubled times, with farmlands untended, settlers abruptly leaving, villas occupied. I was on watch every night, protecting our new house from burglars and thieves. The former proprietors — the Larquais family Mama worked for — had run away three months earlier. So we were the new owners of the place by right of possession. This had come about very simply. One morning we were in our little cubbyhole, which adjoined the main house, when we heard cries, furniture being moved, the sounds of an engine, and more cries. This was in March 1962. I was home because there was no work, and Mama had decreed a sort of emergency law, which had been in force for several weeks: I must remain within a perimeter that she could monitor. I saw her enter her employers' house and after an hour's stay return in tears — but she was crying tears of joy. She informed me that they were all leaving, the whole family, and that we were charged with looking after the house. We were to act as stewards, more or less, and wait for them to return. They never returned. The day after their departure, beginning at dawn, we moved in. I'll always remember those first moments. We were fairly intimidated and hardly dared to occupy the main rooms on the first day, contenting ourselves with settling into the kitchen. Mama served me coffee by the lemon tree in the courtyard, where we'd eaten in silence; our flight from Algiers was finally over. At last, we had arrived somewhere. The second night, we ventured into one of the bedrooms and touched the crockery with awed fingers. Other neighbors were on the alert too, looking out for doors to kick down and houses to occupy. We had to decide, and Mama knew just how to go about it. She pronounced the name of a saint unknown to me, invited two other Arab ladies to call on us, made coffee, swung a smoking censer in every room, and gave me a jacket she'd found in an armoire. And that was the way we celebrated Independence: with a house, a jacket, and a cup of coffee. We remained on our guard in the following days, afraid the owners would return or other people would come and kick us out. We didn't sleep much; we were keeping watch. It was impossible to trust anyone at all. Sometimes at night we'd hear smothered cries, running feet, panting, all sorts of disturbing sounds. House doors were smashed in, and one night I even saw a resistance fighter, a guy well known in these parts, shooting out streetlights so he could plunder the surroundings with complete impunity.

Some of the French who'd stayed were worried, despite the promise of protection they had received. One afternoon they all gathered outside the church in Hadjout, next to the imposing town hall, right in the middle of the main street, to protest the murder of two of their fellows by a pair of overzealous *djounoud*, who I'm sure had joined the resistance just a few days earlier. The murderers were executed by their commander after a summary trial, but that didn't stop violent incidents from continuing to happen. Anyway, that same day I was out in the village, looking for an open shop, and in the little group of anxious Frenchmen assembled there I noticed the man who that very evening, or the next day, or a few days later, I can't remember now, would become my victim. He was wearing the same shirt he'd be wearing the day he died, and he wasn't looking at anyone, he just blended into his group, who were all staring worriedly down the main street. They were waiting for the Algerian officials to arrive and enforce justice. Our eyes met briefly; he lowered his. I wasn't unknown to him, and I too had seen him around, with the Larquais family. No doubt a close friend or a relative who often came to visit them. That afternoon there was a big, heavy, blinding sun in the sky, and the unbearable heat scrambled my mind. Generally I walked at a brisk pace in Hadjout, because nobody could understand why, at my age, I hadn't joined the resistance, which was fighting to liberate the country and chase out all the Meursaults. After stopping in front of the little group of *roumis*, I started back home under the scorching sun—it was creaking slowly across the sky, its light so glaring that it seemed intended for tracking down some fugitive rather than brutally lighting up the earth. I took a stealthy look behind me and saw the Frenchman hadn't moved, he was staring at his shoes, and then I forgot about him. We lived at the edge of the village, just before the fields began, and Mama was waiting for me the way she did every time, unmoving and stone-faced, as though braced to receive some always possible piece of bad news. Night fell, and eventually we went to bed.

It was that muffled noise that woke me up. At first I thought it was a wild boar, or maybe a thief. In the darkness, I knocked softly on the door of my mother's room and then opened it; she was already sitting up in bed, staring at me like a cat. I removed the gun, gently, from the knotted scarves it was concealed in. How did we happen to have it? Pure chance. I'd found it two weeks before, hidden in the rafters of the shed. It was a heavy old revolver that looked like a metal dog with one nostril and gave off a strange odor. I remember its weight that night, not pulling me down to earth but toward some obscure target. I remember I wasn't afraid, though the whole house had suddenly become unfamiliar again. It was almost two in the morning, and only the barking of dogs in the distance marked the frontier between the earth and the night sky. The sound came from the shed, and it already had a smell, and I followed it with Mama close behind me, clutching the rope around my neck more tightly than ever, and when I got to the shed and peered into the darkness, the black shadow suddenly had eyes, then a shirt, the beginnings of a face, and a grimace. The man was there, wedged between two stories and some walls, and his only way out was my story, which left him no chance. He was breathing with difficulty. Of course I remember his eyes, his gaze. To tell the truth, he wasn't looking at me. He seemed hypnotized by the heavy gun in my fist. I think he was so frightened he couldn't be angry at me or reproach me for his death. If he had moved, I would have struck him and laid him out flat, facedown in the night, with bubbles bursting on the surface around his head. But he didn't move, at least not in the beginning. "All I have to do is turn and walk away, and it'll be over," I told myself, not believing it for a moment. Mama was there, forbidding any attempt of mine to dodge away, and demanding what she couldn't obtain with her own hands: revenge.

We exchanged no words, she and I. All of a sudden we tipped over, both of us, into a kind of madness. I'm sure we both thought about Musa at the same time. This was our opportunity to be done with him, to give him a worthy burial. It was as if our lives since Musa's death had been nothing but playacting, a barely serious reprieve, and all we'd really been doing was waiting for that *roumi* to come back on his own, returning to the scene of the crime, which we carried along with us wherever we went. I took a few steps forward, feeling my body stiffen with refusal. I wanted to fight through that resistance, and I took one more step. That was when the Frenchman moved — or maybe he didn't even do that — and retreated into the shadows in the farthest corner of the shed. All I could see was shadow, and every object, every angle and curve stood out so confusedly it insulted my reason.

Because he'd backed away, the darkness devoured what remained of his humanity; all I could see now was his shirt, which reminded me of his empty eyes that morning — or the morning before, I couldn't remember.

It was like two sharp raps on the door of deliverance. That, at least, is what I thought I felt. Afterward? I dragged his body into the courtyard, and then we buried him. It's not as easy to bury a dead man as books and movies would have you believe. The corpse always weighs twice as much as the living person did, refuses the hand you offer it, and adheres with all its blind weight to the surface of the earth, clutching whatever last bit it can reach. The Frenchman weighed a lot, and we had no time. I dragged him about a meter before his reddened, bloody shirt tore. Part of it remained in my hand. I exchanged two or three murmurs with Mama, who seemed already to be elsewhere, not much interested anymore in the universe she bequeathed me like an antique stage set. I used a pick and a shovel and dug a deep hole very close to the lemon tree, the sole witness to the scene. Oddly enough, I felt cold, even though we were in the heart of summer, even though the night was hot and as sensuous as a woman who'd waited too long for love, and I wanted to dig and dig and never stop or raise my head. My mother suddenly snatched up the torn piece of shirt lying on the ground and sniffed at it for a long time. That seemed to give her back her sight at last. Her eyes fell on me, practically surprised.

And after that? Nothing happened. And whereas the night — its trees plunged into the stars for hours, its moon, the last pallid trace of the vanished sun, the door of our little house, which forbade time to enter it, and the blind darkness, our only witness — whereas the night was gently beginning to withdraw its confusion and give things back their angles, my body was able to recognize the arrival of the denouement at last. It made me shiver with an almost animal delight. Lying on my back in the courtyard, I made an even denser night for myself by closing my eyes. When I opened them, I remember seeing yet more stars in the sky, and I knew I was trapped in a bigger dream, a more gigantic denial, that of another being who always kept his eyes closed and didn't want to see anything, like me.

IX

I'm not telling you this story to be absolved a posteriori or to get rid of a bad conscience. At the time when I did that killing, God wasn't as alive and heavy in this country as he is today, and in any case, I'm not afraid of hell. I just feel a kind of weariness, a frequent urge to sleep, and sometimes severe vertigo.

The day after the murder, everything was intact. The insects were chirring as deafeningly as always, and the sun was beating down strong and straight, planted in the heart of the earth. Maybe the only thing that had changed for me was the sensation I've already described to you: At the moment when I committed my crime, I felt a door somewhere was definitively closing on me. I concluded that I had been condemned—and for that, I'd needed neither judge nor God nor the charade of a trial. Only myself.

I'd love to have a trial! And I assure you: Unlike your hero, I'd go on trial with the enthusiasm of a liberated man. I dream about that courtroom full of people. A big room, and Mama there, struck dumb at last, incapable of defending me for lack of a precise language, sitting on a bench in a daze, hardly recognizing her belly or my body. A few idle journalists in the back rows, as well as Larbi, my brother Musa's friend, and especially Meriem, with her thousands of books hovering above her head like butterflies. And then your hero, playing the role of the prosecutor in this unique remake, asking me my family name, my given name, and my ancestry. Joseph, the man I killed, is also present, and my neighbor, the horrible Koran reciter, who comes to my cell to explain to me about how forgiving God is. A grotesque scene, because the background's missing. What could I be accused of, me, who served my mother even after my death, and who buried myself alive before her eyes so she could live in hope? What will my accusers say? That I didn't weep when I killed Joseph? That I went to the movies after firing two shots into his body? No, there were no movies in those days, and the dead were so numerous that nobody wept for them, they were just given a number and two witnesses. I searched vainly for a court and a judge, but I never found them.

All things considered, my life has been more tragic than your hero's. I've interpreted all those roles in turn. Sometimes Musa, sometimes the stranger, sometimes the judge, sometimes the man with the sick dog, the treacherous Raymond, and even the insolent flute player who mocked the murderer. It's essentially a private performance, with me as the sole protagonist. A splendid one-man show. Everywhere in this country, there are cemeteries for foreigners, places where the calm grass is only a façade. All the fine people in there are chattering and jostling one another, intent on resurrection, inserted between the end of the world and the beginning of a trial. There are too many of them! Far too many! No, I'm not drunk, I'm dreaming about a trial, but they're all dead already, and I was the last to kill. The story of Cain and

Abel, but at the end of mankind, not at the start. You understand better now, don't you? This isn't a trite story of forgiveness or revenge, it's a curse, it's a trap.

What I want is to remember. I want it so much and so badly, maybe I could go back in time and get to that summer day in 1962 and make that beach off-limits, for two hours, to every possible Arab in this country. Or I could finally stand trial, yes, and watch the courtroom get crushed by the heat as I do so. Hallucinating, caught between the infinite and the panting of my own body in its cell, striving with muscle and thought against walls and imprisonment. I blame my mother, I lay the blame on her. The truth is, *she* committed that crime. *She* held my arm steady while Musa held hers and so on back to Abel or his brother. I'm philosophizing? Yes, yes I am. Your hero had a good understanding of that sort of thing; whether or not to commit murder is the only proper question for a philosopher, the only one he ought to ask. All the rest is chitchat. However, I'm only a man sitting in a bar. It's the end of the day, the stars are coming out one by one, and the night has already given the sky a positively exhilarating depth. I love this regular denouement; the night calls the earth back to the sky and gives it a portion of infinity almost equal to its own. I killed at night, and ever since I've had night's immensity for an accomplice.

Ah! You look surprised by my language. How and where did I learn it? At school. On my own. With Meriem. She helped me more than anyone to perfect my knowledge of your hero's tongue, and she was the cause of my discovering and reading and rereading the book you carry around in your bag like a fetish. That was how

French became the main tool of a meticulous, maniacal investigation. The two of us used the language like a magnifying glass as we went over the scene of the crime together. And with my tongue and Meriem's mouth, I devoured hundreds of books! It seemed to me I was approaching the places where the murderer had lived, I was holding him by the jacket while he was embarking for nothingness, I was forcing him to turn around, look at me, recognize me, speak to me, respond to me, take me seriously: He trembled with fear at my resurrection, after he'd told the whole world I'd died on a beach in Algiers!

I figure the only trial I'm going to be put on is one I make up for myself right here in this crummy bar, so let me go back to the murder. You're young, but you can serve as judge, prosecutor, public, and journalist... Well, after I'd killed a man, it wasn't my innocence I missed the most, it was the border that had existed until then between my life and crime. That's a line that's hard to redraw later. The Other is a unit of measurement you lose when you kill. Afterward, I often felt an incredible, almost divine giddiness at the thought of somehow resolving every-thing — at least in my daydreams — by committing mur-der. The list of my victims was long. I'd start with one of our neighbors, a self-proclaimed "veteran mujahid," whereas everyone knows he's a crook and a con man who has taken money from the contributions of real muja-hideen and diverted it to his own profit; then comes an insomniac dog, a brown, scrawny, wild-eyed creature that drags its carcass through the streets of my city; next up, a maternal uncle who for years came to see us every Eid, at the end of Ramadan, and promised to repay an

90

old debt, without ever actually doing it; and finally, the first mayor of Hadjout, who treated me like a weakling because I hadn't left to join the resistance like the others. Such thoughts became commonplace with me after I killed Joseph and threw his body down a well—a figure of speech, of course, because, as I've said, I buried him. What's the point of putting up with adversity, suffering, or even an enemy's hatred if you can resolve everything with a few simple gunshots? The unpunished murderer develops a certain inclination to laziness. But there's something irreparable as well: The crime forever compromises both love and the possibility of loving. I killed a man, and since then, life is no longer sacred in my eyes. After what I did, the body of every woman I met quickly lost its sensuality, its possibility of giving me an illusion of the absolute. Every surge of desire was accompanied by the knowledge that life reposes on nothing solid. I could suppress it so easily that I couldn't adore it—I would have been deceiving myself. I'd chilled all human bodies by killing only one. Indeed, my dear friend, the only verse in the Koran that resonates with me is this: "If you kill a single person, it is as if you have killed the whole of mankind."

Say, this morning I read a fascinating article in an old, out-of-date newspaper. It told the story of a certain Sadhu Amar Bharati. I'm sure you've never heard of this gentleman. He's an Indian who claims to have kept his right hand raised toward the sky for thirty-eight years. As a result, his arm's nothing more than a bone covered with skin. It will remain fixed in its position until he dies. Maybe that's how it goes for all of us, basically. For some, it's both arms, embracing the void left behind by a beloved body; for others, it's a hand holding back a child already grown, or a leg raised above a threshold never crossed, or teeth clenched on a word never uttered, et cetera. The idea's been amusing me all day. Why hasn't this Indian ever lowered his arm? According to the article, he's a man of middle-class background, he had a job, a house, a wife, and three children, and he led a normal, peaceful life. One day he received a revelation; his God spoke to him and commanded him to tramp tirelessly through the country and preach world peace, always holding up his right arm. Thirty-eight years later, his arm is petrified. I like this strange anecdote, it resembles the story I'm telling you. More than half a century since the gunshots were fired on the beach, my arm's still raised, impossible to lower, wrinkled, eaten away by time — dry skin on dead bones. Except that's the way I feel about my entire being: All the muscles are gone, but it's stretched out and painful. Because holding this posture doesn't involve merely depriving yourself of a limb, it likewise entails atrocious, piercing pains — although they've disappeared nowadays. Listen to this: "It used to be painful, but I've become used to it now," the Indian declares. The journalist describes his martyr in great detail. The man's arm has lost all feeling. Fixed in a semi-vertical position, it's become atrophied, and the fingernails of his right hand curl around upon themselves. At first, the story made me smile, but now I'm considering it seriously. It's a true story, for I've lived it myself. I've seen Mama's body stiffen into the same strenuous, irreversible pose. I've seen it dry up like that man's useless arm, raised against the force of gravity. Mama is, in fact, a statue. I remember that when she wasn't doing anything, she'd just stay there, sitting on the ground, unmoving, as though devoid of all reason for existence. Oh, yes! Years later, I discovered how much patience she'd had and how she'd hoisted the Arab — that is, me — into that scene, where he was able to take hold of a revolver, execute the *roumi* Joseph, and bury him.

Let's go home, young man. As a general rule, one sleeps better after a confession.

X

The day after my crime, everything was very peaceful. I'd fallen asleep in the courtyard, worn out by grave-digging, and it was the smell of coffee that woke me up. Mama was singing! I remember that very well, because it was the first time she'd allowed herself to sing, even if only sotto voce. You never forget the first day in the world. The lemon tree practically pretended not to have seen anything. I decided I wouldn't go out that day. My mother's nearness, her kindness, her consideration were of the sort reserved for a child prodigy, or a traveler who's finally come home, or a relative given back by the sea, dripping and smiling. She was celebrating Musa's return. So I turned aside when she handed me a cup, and I nearly pushed away her hand, which for an instant had grazed my hair. However, I knew at the very instant when I was rejecting her that I'd never be able to bear having any other body close to mine. I'm exaggerating? Committing a real murder gives one some new, clear-cut certitudes. Read what your hero wrote about his stay in a prison cell. I often reread that passage myself, it's the most interesting part of his whole hodgepodge of sun and salt. When your hero's in his cell, that's when he's best at asking the big questions.

The color of the sky was no concern of mine, so I went back to my room and slept for a few more hours.

Around midday, a hand pulled me out of my sleep. Mama, of course, who else? "They came looking for you," she told me. She wasn't panicked or worried; she figured they couldn't kill her son twice, and I understood that. Some secondary rites still needed to be performed before Musa's story could really end. It was a few minutes after two in the afternoon, I think. I went out into the little courtyard and noticed two empty cups, some cigarette butts, and traces of footsteps in the dirt. Mama explained that the two gunshots in the night had alarmed the *djounoud*. Some people in the neighborhood had pointed to our house, so two soldiers had come to hear our version. My mother said they'd eyed the courtyard vaguely, accepted the cups of coffee, and asked questions about her life and her household. Well, I guessed the rest right away: Mama had put on her show. She told the *djounoud* about Musa and made such an impression on them that they ended up kissing her forehead and assuring her that her son was well and properly avenged, as were millions of others killed by the French every summer afternoon at two o'clock sharp. "A Frenchman disappeared last night," they told her before leaving. "Tell your son to come down to the town hall, the colonel wants to talk to him. You'll get him back. We just have a few questions to ask him." At this point, Mama interrupted her account and examined me. Her little eyes seemed to be asking, "What are you going to do?" Then she lowered her voice and added that she'd made everything vanish, from blood traces to murder weapon. Not far from the lemon tree were a couple of extra-large cowpats…Nothing of the previous night remained, neither sweat nor dust nor echo. The Frenchman had been erased with the same meticulousness applied to the Arab on the beach twenty years earlier. Joseph was a Frenchman, and Frenchmen were dying more or less everywhere in the country at the time, and Arabs likewise, for that matter. Seven years of the national War of Liberation had transformed your guy Meursault's beach into a battlefield.

For my part, I perceived what the new lords of the land really wanted from me. Even if I showed up with the Frenchman's body on my back, my crime wouldn't be the one the eye could see, but that other crime, the one the intuition could guess: my strangeness. Already. I decided not to go down to the town hall that same day. Why not? Not out of bravery, and not by calculation, but only because of the general torpor I found myself in. In the afternoon, the sky looked fabulously rejuvenated, the sight is committed to my memory like a date. I felt light, in balance with the other weights on my heart, and relaxed, and fit for idleness. Equidistant between Musa's grave and Joseph's. You must understand why. An ant ran over my hand. I was nearly stunned by the idea of my own life, the proof of it, its temperature, in contrast with the proof of death, just two meters away from me, there, under the lemon tree. Mama knew the reason why she'd killed, and she was the only one who knew it! Neither Musa nor Joseph nor I was affected by her certitude. I raised my eyes and saw her sweeping the courtyard, bending toward the ground, discussing things with dead relatives or with some ladies, former neighbors who now resided in her head. For one moment, I felt sorry for her. The numbness in my arms became a poignant delight, and I watched the shadows slowly sliding over the walls of our courtyard. Then I fell asleep again.

In fact, I slept for nearly three days straight, a heavy sleep with waking moments that barely revealed to me my own name. I stayed there in my bed, unmoving, without ideas or projects, my body new and amazed. Mama, playing the game of patience, let me alone. Every time I think about those long days of sleep, I find them strange, because outside that courtyard the country was still being torn apart by the celebrations of its freedom. Thousands of Meursaults were running in every direction, and so were Arabs. That meant nothing to me. It was only later, weeks and months afterward, that I started gradually discovering the immensity of both the destruction and the joy.

Ah, you know, I never bothered myself to write a book, and yet I dream of committing one. Just one! No, don't be so sure, it wouldn't be a new investigation into your man Meursault's case. It would be something else, something more intimate. A great treatise on digestion. There it is! A kind of culinary book, combining aromas and metaphysics, spoons and divinities, the people and their bellies. The raw and the cooked. Someone told me recently that the best-selling books in this country are cookbooks. Well, *I* know why. While Mama and I were waking up from our drama, staggering but maybe, finally, appeased, the rest of the country was devouring everything, gobbling up the land and the rest of the sky and the houses and the power poles and the species that couldn't defend themselves. As I see it, my countrymen don't eat exclusively with their hands but with everything else too: with their eyes, feet, tongue, and skin. Everything gets devoured: bread, sweets of all sorts, meats from afar, fowl, all kinds of herbs. But in the end, apparently, that's no longer sufficient. The way I see it, these people need something bigger as a counterweight to the abyss. My mother used to call that "the endless serpent," and I think it'll lead us all to premature death, or to someplace on the edges of the earth where we can topple over into the void. You see? Take a good look at this city and the people here, all around us, and you'll understand. They've been devouring everything in sight for years. Plaster, the well-polished round stones you find on the seashore, the remains of all sorts of posts. As the years have passed, the beast has become less picky and even eats whatever pieces of sidewalk are available. Sometimes it advances right up to the threshold of the desert — which owes its survival only to its blandness, I believe. It's been years now since the animals ceased to exist, reduced to images in books. There are no more forests in this country, none at all. The big, bulky swans' nests have disappeared as well. As a teenager, I never got tired of admiring those nests, perched on the tops of minarets and the last churches. Have you seen the landings in the apartment blocks, the empty living quarters, the walls, the colonists' old wine cellars, all those ruined buildings? They make a meal. I'm rambling again. I wanted to tell you about the first day in the world and here I am, talking about the last one…

What were we talking about? Ah, yes, the days after the crime. Well, as I told you, I didn't do anything, I slept while the people were devouring the incredible country that had been given back to them. Those were days without names or language; I saw people and trees differently, from an unexpected angle, over and above their usual designations; I returned to primordial feeling. For a brief while, I knew your hero's genius: the ability to tear open the common, everyday language and emerge on the other side, where a more devastating language is waiting to narrate the world in another way. That's it! The reason why your hero tells the story of my brother's murder so well is that he'd reached a new territory, a language that was unknown and grew more powerful in his embrace, the words like pitilessly carved stones, a language as naked as Euclidian geometry. I think that's the grand style, when all is said and done: to speak with the austere precision the last moments of your life impose on you. Imagine a dying man and the words he says. That's your hero's genius: He describes the world as if he's going to die at any moment, as if he has to choose his words with an economy of breathing. He's an ascetic.

Five days later, answering the summons I'd received from the country's new leaders, I betook myself to the Hadjout town hall. There I was arrested and thrown into a room that already contained several people—a few Arabs (who doubtless hadn't fought in the revolution or whom the revolution hadn't killed), but mostly Frenchmen; I didn't know any of them, not even by sight. Somebody asked me in French what I'd done. I answered that I was accused of having killed a Frenchman, and they were all silent. Night fell. Bugs tormented me in my sleep the whole night, but I was somewhat used to that. A sunbeam came through the skylight and woke me up. I heard noises in the corridors, footsteps, shouted orders. Nobody gave us any coffee. I waited. The French stared hard at the few Arabs, who scrutinized them in turn. Two *djounoud* eventually came in. When they thrust their chins in my direction, the guard grabbed me by the neck and pulled me outside. I was hustled into a jeep, and I figured I was being transferred to the police station, where they could put me in a cell by myself. The Algerian flag on the jeep flapped in the wind. Along the way, I saw my mother walking on the shoulder of the road, enveloped in her haik. She stopped to let the convoy pass. I smiled at her vaguely, but she remained stone-faced. I'm sure she followed us with her eyes before she started walking again. I was thrown into a cell, where I had a bucket for a toilet and a tin washbasin. The prison was situated in the center of town, and through a small window I could see some cypresses with whitewashed trunks. A guard came in and told me I had a visitor. I thought it must be my mother, and I was right.

I followed the taciturn guard the whole length of an endless corridor that led to a small room. Two *djounoud* were there, completely indifferent to us. They seemed weary, worn, and tense, with slightly crazy eyes, as if seeking the invisible enemy they'd spent years with the resistance on the lookout for. I turned to my mother; her face was closed but serene. She was sitting, straight-backed and dignified, on a wooden bench. The room we were in had two doors: the one I'd come through and another that opened into a second corridor. There I could see two little old French ladies. The first one was dressed all in black, and her lips were tightly closed. The second was a big woman with bushy hair who looked very nervous. I could also see into another room, most likely an office, with open folders, sheets of paper on the floor, and a broken windowpane. All was silent — a little too silent, in fact; it made it hard to find words. I didn't know what to say. I speak very little to my mother, it's been like that forever, and we weren't used to having so many people around, hanging on our lips. Only one person had ever intruded on us, couple that we were, and I'd killed him. Here I had no weapon. Mama leaned toward me abruptly and I flinched hard, as if I might be struck in the face or devoured in one gulp. She spoke very fast: "I told him you were my only son and that was why you couldn't join the resistance." After a silent pause, she added: "I told them Musa died." She was still talking about his death as if it had happened yesterday, or as if the date was a mere detail. She explained that she'd shown the colonel the two scraps of newspaper with the article about an Arab killed on a beach. The colonel had hesitated to believe her. No names were given, and there was nothing to prove she was really the mother of a martyr; and besides, could he even have *been* a martyr, since the crime dated from 1942? I told her, "It's difficult to prove." The fat Frenchwoman seemed to be following our discussion with tremendous concentration. I believe everyone was listening to us. Granted, there was nothing else to do. You could hear the birds outside, the sounds of engines, of trees reaching out to embrace in the wind, but none of that was very interesting. I had no idea what I could add. "I didn't bawl like the other women. I think he believed me because of that," she said in one urgent breath, as if murmuring a secret. However, I had already understood what she was really trying to tell me, and besides, the conversation was over.

I had the impression that everybody was waiting for an honorable exit, a sign, a snap of the fingers to wake them up, some way of closing the interview without looking ridiculous. I felt an immense weight on my shoulders. The meeting between a mother and an incarcerated son must end either in a tender embrace or in tears. And maybe one of us should have said something... But nothing was said, and the time seemed to drag on interminably. Then we heard the squealing of tires outside. My mother sprang nimbly to her feet. Out in the corridor, the old woman with the tight lips took the beginnings of a step. One of the soldiers came up to me and put his hand on my shoulder, the other coughed discreetly. The two Frenchwomen were staring at the end of the corridor, which I couldn't see, I could just hear footsteps echoing down the hall. As they drew closer, I saw the two old women turn pale and shrink back with distorted faces, all the while shooting each other panicked looks. "It's him, he speaks French," the bigger of the two women said, pointing at me. Mama whispered, "The colonel believed me. When you get out, I'll find you a wife." Now there was a promise I wasn't expecting. But I understood what she meant to say by it. Then I was brought back to my cell. Once inside, I sat down and looked out at the cypresses. All sorts of ideas were colliding in my head, but I felt calm, and I remembered Bab-el-Oued and our wanderings there, Mama's and mine, our arrival here in this town, the light, the sky, the swans' nests. In Hadjout I learned to hunt birds, but that ceased to amuse me as the years passed. Why didn't I ever take up arms and join the resistance? Yes, that's what you were obligated to do in those days, when you were young and you couldn't go swimming. I was twenty-seven, and nobody in the village was able to understand why I hung around instead of going underground and joining "the brothers." People in Hadjout had been making fun of me for a long time, ever since our arrival there. They thought I was sick or lacking male private parts or a prisoner of the woman who called herself my mother. When I was fifteen, I had to kill a dog with my own hands, using a blade fashioned from the lid of a sardine can, to make the boys of my age stop laughing at me and calling me a coward and a wimp. One day a man who was watching me play kickball in the street with some other kids suddenly called out, "Your legs don't match." At my mother's insistence, I went to school, and very quickly I made enough progress to read her the fragments of newspapers she collected, with articles that told the story of how Musa had been killed but never gave his name, his neighborhood, his age, or even his initials. The truth is, we started the war — in a way — before the people did. Of course, I didn't kill a Frenchman until July 1962, but our family had known death, martyrdom, exile, flight, hunger, grief, and pleas for justice at a time when the country's war leaders were still playing marbles and lugging baskets in the markets in Algiers.

So at the age of twenty-seven, I was a sort of anomaly. And sooner or later, I'd have to answer for it before an officer in the Army of National Liberation. Meanwhile time passed in the sky I could see through the window, and it passed in the color of the trees, which became dark and murmurous. The guard brought me a meal and I thanked him, and then I thought it would be a great pleasure to sleep some more. I felt thoroughly free in my cell, without Mama or Musa. Before leaving me alone, the guard turned around and fired a question at me: "Why didn't you help the brothers?" He said it without nastiness, with kindness even, and with a certain curiosity. I didn't collaborate with the colonists and everyone in the village knew it, but I wasn't a mujahid either, and it bothered a great many people that I was sitting there in the middle, in that intermediary state, as if I was taking a nap under a rock on the beach or kissing a beautiful young woman's breasts while my mother was getting robbed or raped. "They're going to ask you that," the guard threw out before closing the cell door. I knew what he was talking about. Afterward I slept, but before that, I listened. It was all I had to do, I didn't smoke, and I hadn't minded when they took my shoelaces and my belt and everything I had in my pockets. I didn't want to kill time. I don't like that expression. I like to look at time, follow it with my eyes, take what I can. For once, there was no corpse on my back! I decided to enjoy my idleness. Did I think about how badly the next day could turn out? A little, no doubt, but I didn't dwell on it. Death was something I was strangely used to. I could move from the living to the deceased, from the hereafter to the sun, just by changing the given names: Harun (my name), Musa, Meursault, or Joseph. According to preference, almost. In the first days of Independence, death was as gratuitous, absurd, and unexpected as it had been on a sunny beach in 1942. I could be accused of anything, my chances of being shot as an example or set free with a kick in the butt were just about equal, and I knew it. Then evening came along with a handful of stars, and the darkness dug a hole in my cell, blurred the outlines of the walls, and brought a sweet smell of grass. It was still summer, and by peering into the blackness I was eventually able to glimpse a bit of the moon, which was slowly sliding my way. I slept again, for a very long time, while unseen trees tried to walk, flailing about with their big branches in the effort to free their black, fragrant trunks. My ear was glued to the ground of their struggle.

XI

They questioned me several times, but it was just so they could find out who I was, and the sessions never took very long.

At the police station, no one seemed to be interested in my case. Nevertheless, an officer in the Army of National Liberation eventually received me. He looked me over with curiosity and asked me several questions: name, address, occupation, date and place of birth. I answered politely. He was quiet for a moment, seemed to be looking for something in a notebook, and then he fixed his gaze on me again, this time with hardened eyes, and asked, "You know Monsieur Larquais?" I didn't want to lie—I didn't need to. I knew I wasn't there for having committed a murder but for not having done so at the right moment. I'm summing it up like that to make it easier for you to understand. I gave a smart-ass reply: "Some people used to know him, I believe." The man was young, but the war had aged him—unevenly, if I may say so. His face, now stiff and stern, was wrinkled in places, but I could tell he had some vigorous muscles under his shirt, and his skin showed the suntan people get when they have nothing but holes and maquis to hide in. He smiled at my attempt to evade him. "I'm not asking for the truth. Nobody needs that here. If it turns out you killed him, you'll pay." He burst out laughing. His laughter was big, powerful, booming, incredible. "Who would've thought I'd have to judge an Algerian for the murder of a Frenchman?" he asked between guffaws. He was right. As I well knew, I wasn't there for having killed Joseph Larquais, nor would I be, not even if Joseph Larquais came there in person to accuse me, flanked by two witnesses and flaunting the two bullets I fired into his body in the palm of one hand, with his shirt rolled up under his armpits. I was there because I'd killed him all by myself, and for no good reason. "You understand?" the officer asked me. I said I did.

They brought me back to my cell so the officer could go to lunch. I did nothing and waited. I was sitting down, not thinking about very much. One leg lolled, as if posing, in a pool of sunlight. The skylight held the whole sky. I could hear distant conversations and the sounds of trees. I wondered what Mama was doing. She must surely be sweeping the courtyard, I thought, and conversing with all her family and friends. At two o'clock in the afternoon, the door opened and I was taken to the colonel's office once again. He was waiting for me, calmly sitting under the huge Algerian flag that was hanging on the wall. A revolver lay on the corner of his desk. They had me sit on a chair, where I remained unmoving. The officer didn't say anything, letting a heavy silence settle over us. I suppose he wanted to act on my nerves, to get me upset. I smiled, because that was a bit like the method Mama used when she wanted to punish me. "You're twenty-seven," he began, and then he leaned toward me with fire in his eyes, pointing an accusing finger. He shouted, "So why didn't you take up arms to liberate your country? Answer me! Why?" His features struck me as vaguely comical.

He stood up, violently yanked a drawer open, pulled out a little Algerian flag, came over to me, and waved it under my nose. In a threatening and rather nasal voice, he said, "Do you know what this is? Do you?" I replied, "Yes, of course." Then he launched into a patriotic rant, reiterating his faith in his independent country and in the sacrifice made by one and a half million martyrs. "This Frenchman, you should have killed him with us, during the war, not last week!" I didn't see what difference that made, I replied. Visibly taken aback, he was silent for a while, and then he roared, "It makes all the difference!" He gave me a dirty look. I asked what the difference was. He started stammering, declaring that killing and making war were not the same thing, that we weren't murderers but liberators, that nobody had given me orders to kill that Frenchman, and that I should have done it *before*. "Before what?" I asked. "Before July 5! Yes, before, not after, damn it!" There were a few sharp raps on the door, and then a soldier entered and placed an envelope on the desk. This interruption seemed to exasperate the colonel. The soldier gave me a quick glance and withdrew. "Well?" the officer said. I replied that I didn't understand, and I asked him, "If I killed Monsieur Larquais on the fifth of July at two o'clock in the morning, are we supposed to say the war was still going on, or had Independence already come? Was it *before* or *after*?" The officer sprang up like a jack-in-the-box, reached out a surprisingly long arm, and dealt me a monumental slap in the face. I felt my cheek go icy cold, then fiery hot, and my eyes got involuntarily moist. I had to straighten my spine. After that, nothing happened. We remained where we were, both of us, face-to-face. The colonel's arm slowly returned to its place by his side, and I probed the inside of my cheek with my tongue. We heard a voice in the corridor, and the officer used the opportunity to break the silence: "Is it true that your brother was killed by a Frenchman?" I said yes, but that was before the revolution broke out. The colonel suddenly looked very tired. "It should simply have been done before," he murmured, almost pensively. "There are rules to obey," he added, as if to convince himself of the soundness of his reasoning. He asked me to tell him again exactly what my occupation was. "I'm a government official. Land Administration," I told him. "A useful profession for the nation," he muttered, as though to himself. Then he asked me to tell him Musa's story, but his mind seemed to be on something else. I told him what I knew, which is to say, not much. The officer listened to me distractedly and then concluded that my tale was a bit thin, not to say improbable. "Your brother's a martyr, but you, I don't know…" I found this way of putting it incredibly profound.

Somebody brought him a cup of coffee, and he dismissed me. As I was leaving the room, he rapped out, "We know all about you, you and all the others. Don't forget that." I didn't know how to answer, so I didn't say anything. Back in my cell, I started feeling chagrined. I knew I was going to be released, and the knowledge cooled the strange ardor boiling inside me. The walls seemed to close in, the skylight shrank, all my senses panicked. The night was going to be bad, dull, suffocating. I tried to think about pleasant things such as swans' nests, but nothing worked. They were going to set me free without explanation, whereas I wanted to be sentenced. I wanted to be relieved of the heavy shadow that was turning my life into darkness. There was even something unjust about their letting me go like that, without explaining whether I was a criminal, a murderer, a dead man, a victim, or simply an undisciplined moron. I found their casual attitude toward my crime almost insulting. I had killed, the thought made me incredibly dizzy. Yet basically nobody had anything bad to say about that. Only the timing seemed to pose a vague problem. What negligence, what flippancy! Didn't they see they were disqualifying my act, obliterating it, by treating it like that? The gratuitousness of Musa's death was unconscionable. And now my revenge had just been struck down to the same level of insignificance!

The next day they released me, without a word, at dawn, the moment soldiers often choose for making a decision. Some suspicious *djounoud* were muttering behind my back, as if they were still in the underground even though the whole country belonged to them. They were young peasants from the mountains, and their eyes were hard. I think the colonel had decided that I was to live in the shame of my alleged cowardice. He believed I was going to suffer for it. He was, of course, wrong. Ha, ha! I'm still laughing about it today. He deluded himself totally, totally...

By the way, do you know why Mama chose Joseph Larquais as the sacrificial victim—because you can say she chose him, yes you can, even though he came to us that night? It's hardly plausible, I promise you. She explained it to me the day after the crime, while I was half asleep between two oblivious naps. Ah well, that *roumi* had to be punished, according to Mama, because he loved to go for a swim at two in the afternoon! He'd come back tanned, lighthearted, happy, and free. Once he came back to Hadjout, paid a visit to the Larquais family, and displayed that same happiness, which Mama, though busying herself with her housekeeping tasks, did not fail to find outrageous…"I'm uneducated, but I understand everything," she declared. "I knew it!" *I knew it.* Knew what, exactly? God alone knows, my friend. But incredible all the same, right? He died because he loved the sea and was always too lively when he came back from it, according to Mama. A genuine madwoman! And I swear to you, this story has not been invented by the wine we're sharing. Unless I dreamed that confession of hers sometime during the long hours of stupefied sleep that followed my crime. Maybe I did, after all. But nevertheless, I can't believe she made up everything. She knew almost all there was to know about him. His age, his appetite for young girls' breasts, his work in Hadjout, and his connection with the Larquais family, which didn't seem to appreciate him very much. "The Larquaises used to say he was a selfish, rootless man who didn't care about anybody. One day their car broke down and they were on the side of the road, waiting for help, when he came driving by, and do you know what he did? He pretended not to see them and continued on his way. As if he had an appointment with God himself. That's what Madame Larquais told me!" I don't remember everything, but I assure you, I could write an entire book on the subject of that *roumi*. "I never served him anything whatsoever. He hated me."

Poor Joseph. The poor guy fell into a well and landed in our courtyard that night. What lunacy. Such gratuitous deaths. Who could take life seriously afterward? Everything in my life seems gratuitous. Even you, with your writing pads and your notes and your books.

Go ahead, go on, I can tell you're dying to, call him over, invite the ghost to join us. I've got nothing more to hide.

XII

I find love inexplicable. The sight of a couple always surprises me, their inevitable slow rhythm, their insistent groping, their indistinguishable food, their way of taking hold of each other with hands and eyes at the same time, their way of blurring at the edges. I can't understand why one hand has to clasp another and never let it go in order to give someone else's heart a face. How do people who love each other do it? How can they stand it? What is it that makes them forget they were born alone and will die separate? I've read many books, and I've concluded that love's an accommodation, certainly not a mystery. It seems to me that the feelings love elicits in other people are, well, pretty much the same as the ones death elicits in me: the sensation that every life is precarious and absolute, the rapid heartbeat, the distress before an unresponsive body. Death—when I received it, when I gave it—is for me the only mystery. All the rest is nothing but rituals, habits, and dubious bonding.

To tell the truth, love is a heavenly beast that scares the hell out of me. I watch it devour people, two by two; it fascinates them with the lure of eternity, shuts them up in a sort of cocoon, lifts them up to heaven, and then drops their carcasses back to earth like peels. Have you seen what becomes of people when they split up? They're scratches on a closed door. Would you like some more wine? Oran! We're in wine country here, it's the last region in Algiers where you'll find any. The vineyards have been uprooted everywhere else. Our server doesn't speak Oranian very well, but he's used to me. He's a force of nature who contents himself with grumbling when he serves you. I'll just signal him...

Meriem. Yes. There was Meriem. It was the summer of 1963. Of course I loved her company, of course I loved to look up from the bottom of my well and see her face suddenly appear in the circle of the sky. I know that if Musa hadn't killed me — actually, it was Musa, Mama, and your hero, those are my three murderers — I would have had a better life, at peace with my language on a little patch of land somewhere in this country, but that wasn't my destiny. As for Meriem, she was very much alive. Can you picture us? Me holding her hand, Musa holding my other hand, Mama perched on my back, and your hero, loitering on all the beaches where we might have celebrated our wedding. An entire family, already hanging on Meriem like a cheap suit.

God, how lovely she was, with her bright smile and her short hair! It pained my heart to be only her shadow and not her reflection. You know, Musa's death and the living grief it imposed on me altered my sense of propriety very early on. A stranger possesses nothing — and I was one. I've never held anything in my hands very long, I start to feel revulsion for it, I have the sensation of excessive weight. Meriem. A beautiful name, don't you think? I wasn't able to keep her.

Take a good look at this city. Like a sort of tumbledown, inefficient hell. It's laid out in circles. In the center, the hard core: the Spanish façades, the Ottoman walls, the buildings the colonists put up, the administrative offices and roads that were built right after Independence; then you've got the oil wells and their surrounding architecture of wholesale relocation; and finally, the shantytowns. And beyond them? Purgatory, I imagine. Inhabited by the millions of people who have died in this country, for this country, because of it, against it, trying to leave it or enter it. I have a neurotic's vision, I'll grant you that...I sometimes think newborn infants are the dead of days gone by, come back like ghosts to reclaim their due.

Is he refusing to answer you or what? Well, you have to find the right formula, I don't know it myself. Don't be intimidated by his newspaper clippings and his philosopher's forehead. Insist. You sure figured out how to go about it with me, didn't you?

XIII

Well, I would have preferred to tell you all these things in their proper order. It would have been better for your future book, but too bad, you'll be able to sort it out.

My schooling took place in the 1950s. A bit late, in other words. When I got admitted to school, I was already a head taller than the other kids. It was a priest—along with Monsieur Larquais—who had insisted to Mama that I should go to the school in Hadjout. I'll never forget the first day, and can you guess why? Because of the shoes. I didn't have any. For the first days of class, I wore a tarboosh and Arab trousers…and I was barefoot. There were two of us, two Arabs, and we were both barefoot. It still makes me laugh today. The teacher pretended not to notice, and I've been grateful to him ever since. He inspected our fingernails, our hands, our notebooks, and our clothes, but he avoided any reference to our feet. I was nicknamed "Sitting Bull" after an Indian chief in a movie that was showing in those days. I spent most of my time sitting around, dreaming of a country where people walked on their hands. I shone in school, I was brilliant. The French language fascinated me like a puzzle, and beyond it lay the solution to the dissonances of my world. I wanted to translate it for Mama, my world, and make it less unjust somehow.

I learned to read, not because I wanted to talk like the others but because I wanted to find a murderer, though

I didn't admit that to myself in the beginning. At first, I could barely decipher the two newspaper clippings Mama kept religiously folded in her bosom, the two reports on the murder of "the Arab." The more I gained confidence in my reading, the more I formed the habit of transforming the content of the articles and embellishing the narrative of Musa's death. Mama would regularly hand me the clippings and say, "Here, take another look, see if they don't say something else, something you didn't understand before." That went on for almost ten years, that routine. I know, because those two texts are printed on my brain. Musa appears in them in the form of two slender initials, and then the journalist doles out a few lines on the criminal and the circumstances of the murder. Just try to imagine the level of genius required to take a local news item two paragraphs long and transform it into a tragedy, describing the famous beach and the scene, grain by grain. I've always loathed its insulting brevity — how could so little importance be accorded to a dead man? Now what more can I tell you? Your hero entertained himself with a newspaper clipping he found in his cell, while *I* got a couple of clippings thrust under my nose every time Mama had a crisis.

Oh, what a joke! Do you understand now? Do you understand why I laughed the first time I read your hero's book? There I was, expecting to find my brother's last words between those covers, the description of his breathing, his features, his face, his answers to his murderer; instead I read only two lines about an Arab. The word "Arab" appears twenty-five times, but not a single name, not once. The first time Mama saw me printing the first letters of the alphabet in my new school notebook, she handed me the two newspaper articles and commanded me to read them. I couldn't, I didn't know how. "It's your brother!" she shot at me in a tone of reproach, as if I'd failed to recognize a body in a morgue. I remained silent. What could I add to that? All of a sudden, I saw what she expected me to do: to make Musa live after dying in his place. A fine brief, don't you think? With two paragraphs, I had to find a body, some alibis, and some accusations. It was a way of continuing Mama's investigations, her search for Zujj, my twin. That led to a strange book—which I perhaps should have written out, as a matter of fact, if I'd had your hero's gift—a counter-investigation. I crammed everything I could between the lines of those two brief newspaper items, I swelled their volume until I made them a cosmos. And so Mama got a complete imaginary reconstruction of the crime, including the color of the sky, the circumstances, the words exchanged between the victim and his murderer, the atmosphere in the court-room, the policemen's theories, the cunning of the pimp and the other witnesses, the lawyers' pleas...Well, I can talk about it like that now, but at the time it was an incredibly disordered jumble, a kind of *Thousand and One Nights* of lies and infamy. Sometimes I felt guilty about it, but most often I was proud. I was giving my mother what she'd searched for in vain in the cemeteries and European neighborhoods of Algiers. That production—an imaginary book for an old woman who had no words—lasted a long time. It came in cycles, don't get me wrong. We wouldn't talk about it for months, but then, all of a sudden, she'd start fidgeting and mumbling, and she'd end up planting herself in front of me and brandishing the two crumpled scraps of newspaper. Sometimes I felt like a ridiculous medium communicating between Mama and a phantom book; she'd ask it questions, and I was supposed to translate its answers.

So that's how my language learning was marked by death. Of course, I read other books, history, geography, but everything had to be related to our family history, to my brother's murder on that blasted beach. That was a mug's game that stopped only sometime in the last months before Independence; maybe my mother could sense Joseph's presence — he was still alive then. Maybe she could make out his mad footsteps as he prowled around Hadjout, around his own future grave, in his beach sandals. I had exhausted all the resources of the language and my imagination. We had no other choice than to wait. For something to happen. To wait for the famous night when a terrorized Frenchman would wind up in our dark courtyard. Yes, I killed Joseph because I had to counterbalance the absurdity of our situation. What happened to those two newspaper clippings? God knows. Maybe they crumbled into dust, maybe they were folded and refolded so many times they dissolved. Or maybe Mama eventually threw them away. I would surely have been inspired enough to write out everything I made up back then, but I didn't have the resources to do it, nor did I realize that the crime could become a book and the victim a simple ricochet of bright light. Is that my fault?

So you can guess the effect it had on us when a young woman with very short, dark brown hair knocked on our door one day and asked a question nobody had ever asked before: "Is this the family home of Musa Uld el-Assas?" It was a Monday in March 1963. The country was in full celebration mode, but a kind of fear underlay the rejoicing, for the beast fattened on seven years of war had become voracious and refused to go back underground. A muted power struggle was raging among the conquering commanders.

"Is this the family home of Musa Uld el-Assas?"

MERIEM

I often repeat that question to myself and try to recapture the cheerful tone she asked it in—very polite and friendly, like a luminous proof of innocence.

It was my mother who opened the door—I wasn't far away, lounging in a corner of the courtyard, I couldn't be bothered to get up—and I was surprised to hear the caller's clear, womanly voice. No one had ever come to pay us a visit. Mama and I constituted a couple that discouraged all forms of sociability, and people avoided me in particular. I was a somber, taciturn bachelor, perceived as a coward. I hadn't fought in the revolution, and that fact was remembered with rancor and tenacity. The strangest thing, however, was to hear Musa's name spoken by a person other than my mother—I myself always said "him." The two newspaper clippings referred to him only with his initials—or maybe not, I don't remember. So anyway, I heard Mama answer "Who?" and then she listened to a long explanation I missed most of. "Better say that to my son," Mama declared, and she invited the visitor inside.

It was high time for me to get up and see who'd come calling. And so I saw her: a small thin woman with dark green eyes, a guileless, white-hot sun. Her beauty hurt my heart. I felt my chest imploding. Until that moment, I'd never looked at a woman as one of life's possibilities. I had enough to do, what with extracting myself from Mama's womb, burying the dead, and killing fugitives. You see what I mean? We lived as recluses, I'd grown used to it, and then all of a sudden this young woman shows up, poised to sweep all before her, everything, my life, the world Mama and I had. I felt ashamed, I got scared. "My name is Meriem," she said. Mama had her sit on a stool, her skirt hiked up a little, I tried not to look at her legs. She explained to me in French that she was a teacher, and she was working on a book that told my brother's story, and the book was written by his murderer.

We were there in the courtyard, Mama and I, speechless, trying to understand what it all meant. Musa was rising from the dead, in a way, stirring in his grave and obliging us once again to feel the heavy sorrow that was his legacy. Meriem sensed our confusion and repeated her explanations slowly, kindly, and also a bit cautiously. She addressed Mama and me in turn, murmuring as though we were convalescents. We remained silent, but eventually I came out of my trance and asked some questions that couldn't hide how flustered I was.

In fact, I think I felt as though a sixth and final bullet had just pierced a new hole in my brother's skin. And that's how Musa my brother died three times in a row. The first time was at two o'clock in the afternoon on "the day of the beach"; the second time, when I had to dig him an empty grave; and the third and last time, when Meriem entered our lives.

I vaguely recall the scene: Mama suddenly on the alert, her eyes mad and staring, herself coming and going under the pretext of making more tea or looking for the sugar, the shadows spreading on the walls, Meriem's discomfort. "I had the impression I'd showed up with my tale and my questions and interrupted a funeral," she admitted to me later, after we started seeing each other — unbeknownst to Mama, naturally. Before she left, she took the famous little volume out of her bag, the same work you so sensibly keep in your briefcase. In her view, the thing was very simple. A celebrated author had told the story of an Arab's death and made it into an over-whelming book — "like a sun in a box" was the way she put it, I remember that. She'd been intrigued by the mystery of the Arab's identity, had decided to conduct her own investigation, and by sheer pugnacity had followed the trail back to us. "Months and months of knocking on doors and questioning all kinds of people, just so I could find you," she told me with a disarming smile. And she made a date with me for the next day, at the train station.

I was in love with her from the first second, and I hated her instantly too, for having come into my world like that, tracking a dead man, upsetting my equilibrium. Good God, what a wretch I was!

XIV

So Meriem came in and explained herself, speaking in a soft, gentle tone that held us in thrall as though we were hypnotized. It had taken her months to locate the beginning of our trail in Bab-el-Oued, where practically no one remembered us. She was preparing a thesis — like you, in fact — on your hero and that strange book of his, wherein he tells a murder story with the genius of a mathematician examining a dead leaf. She'd wanted to find the Arab's family, that's what had led her to us after a long investigation on the other side of the mountain, in the country of the living.

Then, guided by I don't know what instinct, Meriem waited until Mama left us for a few minutes before showing me the book. It was a short book in a pretty small format. The cover reproduced a watercolor of a man wearing a suit, hands in his pockets, half turning his back to the sea in the background. Pale colors, indecisive pastels. That's what I remember about it. The title of the book was *The Other*, and the murderer's name was written in severe black letters on the top right: Meursault. But I was distracted, unsettled by that woman's presence. I ventured to look at her hair, her hands, and her neck while she was exchanging some courteous small talk with Mama, who'd come back in from the kitchen. Ever since then, I think, I've liked observing women from the back,

I like the promise of a hidden face and a body you can't discern. I even caught myself—me, who had no knowledge of the subject whatsoever—trying to think up an imaginary name for her scent. One thing I noticed right away was her lively, penetrating intelligence, which was combined with a sort of innocence. Later she told me she was from the east, from Constantine. She claimed the status of a "free woman"—and she accompanied that declaration with a look of defiance that spoke volumes about her resistance to her family's conservatism.

Yes, right, I'm rambling again. You want me to talk about the book, about my reaction when I saw it? To tell you the truth, that episode...I don't know how to start telling you about it. Meriem left, taking away her smell, the nape of her neck, her grace, and her smile, and I was already thinking about tomorrow. Mama and I were both dazed. We had just discovered, all at once, the last traces of Musa's footsteps, his murderer's name—which we had never known—and his exceptional fate. "Everything was written!" Mama blurted out, and I was surprised by the involuntary aptness of her words. *Written*, yes, but in the form of a book, and not by some god. Did we feel ashamed of our stupidity? Did we contain an irrepressible urge to laugh like fools, us, the ridiculous pair stationed in the wings of a masterpiece we didn't even know existed? The whole world knew the murderer, his face, his look, his portrait, and even his clothes, except...the two of us! The Arab's mother and her son, the pathetic Land Administration functionary. Two poor, pitiful natives who had read nothing and put up with everything. Like donkeys. We spent the night avoiding each other's eyes.

God, it was painful to find out we were idiots! The night was long. Mama cursed the young woman and then fell silent. As for me, I was thinking about her breasts and her lips, the way they moved like living fruit. The following morning, Mama shook me awake brutally, bent over me like a threatening old sorceress, and issued her order: "If she comes back, don't open the door!" I had seen that coming, and I knew why she said it. But I was ready for her, I was prepared to respond.

As you will guess, my friend, I obviously did no such thing. I went out early, skipping the usual cup of coffee. As Meriem and I had agreed, I waited for her outside the Hadjout train station, and when I saw her arriving in the bus from Algiers, it was like a hole in my heart. Her presence alone wouldn't be enough to ease my longing. When we found ourselves face-to-face, I felt clumsy and gauche. She smiled at me, first with her eyes, then with her wide, radiant mouth. I stammered as I told her I wanted to know more about the book, and we started walking.

And that lasted for weeks, for months, for centuries.

I'm sure you get it. I was about to experience what Mama's vigilance had always managed to neutralize: incandescence, desire, dreaminess, expectation, the madness of the senses. That's what French books of days gone by refer to as *le tourment*, "the pangs." I can't describe the forces that take hold of your body when you fall in love, which in my vocabulary is a hazy and imprecise word, a myopic millipede crawling up the back of something huge. The book, of course, served as a pretext. *The* book and, later, other books. Meriem showed it to me again and patiently explained, that time and all the other times we saw each other, the context it was written in, its success, the books it inspired, and the infinity of commentaries on every one of its chapters. It all made my head spin.

But on that particular day, the second of our acquaintance, what I mostly looked at were her fingers on the pages of the book, her red nails sliding across the paper, and I forbade myself to think about what she would say if I took hold of her hands. Which was, however, the very thing I wound up doing. And it made her laugh. She knew that at that particular moment, Musa wasn't very important to me. For once. We parted in the early afternoon, and she promised she'd come back. But before going, she asked me what research she would have to do, where she should look, to prove that Mama and I really were the Arab's family. That was an old problem for us, I explained, because we barely had a family name...The remark made her laugh again, but I was hurt. So then I headed for my office. I hadn't even thought about how people would react to my absence! I didn't give a damn, my friend.

And of course, that very evening, I began to read that wretched book. My reading progressed slowly, but I was held as if spellbound. At one and the same time, I felt insulted and revealed to myself. I spent the whole night reading that book. My heart was pounding, I was about to suffocate, it was like reading a book written by God himself. A veritable shock, that's what it was. Everything was there except the essential thing: Musa's name! Nowhere to be found. I counted and recounted, the word "Arab" appeared twenty-five times, but no name, not for any of us. Nothing at all, my friend. Only salt and dazzle and some reflections on the condition of a man charged with a divine mission. Meursault's book didn't teach me anything about Musa except that he had no name, not even at the last moment of his life. On the other hand, it let me see into the murderer's soul as if I were his angel. I found weirdly distorted memories in there, such as the description of the beach, the fabulously lit hour of the murder, the old bungalow that was never found, the days of his trial, and the hours spent in his cell while my mother and I were wandering the streets of Algiers, looking for Musa's body. This man, your writer, seemed to have stolen my twin Zujj, my own description, and even the details of my life and my memories of my interrogation! I read almost the whole night through, laboriously, word by word. It was a perfect joke. I was looking for traces of my brother in the book, and what I found there instead was my own reflection, I discovered I was practically the murderer's double. I finally came to the last lines in the book: "...had only to wish that there be a large crowd of spectators the day of my execution and that they greet me with cries of hate." God, how I would have wanted that! There was a large crowd of spectators, of course, but for his crime, not for his trial. And what spectators! Adoring fans, idolaters! No cries of hate ever came from that throng of admirers. Those last lines overwhelmed me. A masterpiece, my friend. A mirror held up to my soul and to what would become of me in this country, between Allah and ennui.

I didn't sleep that night, as you may imagine. I watched the sky beside the lemon tree.

I didn't show the book to Mama. She would have made me read it over and over, endlessly, right up until

Judgment Day, I swear to you. At sunrise I tore the cover off and hid the book in a corner of the shed. Naturally, I didn't talk to Mama about my date with Meriem the day before, but she detected in my eyes the presence of another woman in my blood. Meriem never came back to our house. I saw her fairly regularly during the following weeks — it lasted all summer, in fact. We agreed that I'd go to the station every day for the arrival of the bus from Algiers. When she could get away, we'd spend a few hours together, walking, idling, sometimes lying under a tree, never for very long. If she didn't come, I'd turn on my heels and go back to work. I started to hope the book would prove to be inexhaustible, would become infinite, so that she'd keep leaning her shoulder against my chest in delight. I told her about almost everything: my childhood, the day of Musa's death, our illiterate and idiotic investigation, the empty grave in El-Kettar cemetery, and the strict rules of our family mourning. The only secret I hesitated to share with her was Joseph's murder. She taught me to read the book in a certain way, tilting it sideways as though to make invisible details fall out. She gave me other books written by that man, and others besides, which allowed me to understand, little by little, how your hero saw the world. Meriem slowly explained to me his beliefs and his fabulous, solitary images. I gathered that he was a sort of orphan who had recognized a sort of fatherless twin in the world and who had suddenly acquired the gift of brotherhood, precisely because of his solitude. I didn't grasp everything, sometimes Meriem seemed to be speaking to me from another planet, she had a voice I loved to hear. And I loved her, deeply.

Love. What a strange feeling, right? It's like being drunk. You've lost your balance, your senses are dulled, but you've got this oddly precise and totally useless insight.

From the very beginning, because I was a wretch, I knew our romance would come to an end, knew I could never hope to keep her in my life. But for the time being, I wanted only one thing: to hear her breathing beside me. Meriem had guessed my state and found it amusing for a while before she realized the depth of my despair. Was that what scared her off? I believe so. Or else she just gradually got tired, I didn't amuse her anymore, she'd exhausted the possibilities of the rather new and exotic path I represented, my "case" stopped being entertaining. I'm bitter, that's wrong. She didn't reject me, I swear to you. On the contrary, I even think she felt a kind of love for me. But she contented herself with loving my disappointment in love, so to speak, and with giving my sorrow the nobility of a precious object, and then, just as a kingdom was beginning to fall into place for me, she went away. Ever since, I've betrayed women methodically and saved the best of myself for the partings. That's the first law inscribed on my tablet of life. Do you want to note down my definition of love? It's pompous but sincere, I concocted it all by myself. Love is kissing someone, sharing their saliva, and going back all the way to the obscure memory of your own birth. I therefore operated as a widower, which adds to one's appeal and attracts the tender feelings of the unwary female. I've been approached by unhappy women and by others too young to understand.

After Meriem left me, I read the book again, and then again. Over and over. Looking to find traces of her in it, her way of reading, her conscientious intonation. Strange, isn't it? To go on a quest for life through the glittering proof of a death! But I'm rambling again, these digressions must be annoying. And yet...

One day we were relaxing under a tree at the edge of the village. Mama pretended ignorance, but she knew I was seeing the girl who'd come from the city to dig around in our cemeteries. Our relationship had changed, Mama's and mine, and I felt a dull temptation to commit some definitively brutal act that would free me from her, monster that she was. My hand brushed against Meriem's breasts, almost by accident. I was drowsing in the broiling shade of the tree, and she had laid her head on my thighs. She arched her back a little to look up at me. Her hair was in her eyes, and she burst into a warbling laugh filled with the lights of another life. I leaned over her face. It was nice, and, sort of joking around, I kissed her on the mouth, canceling the smile on her parted lips. She didn't say anything and I stayed in that bent-over position. I had the whole sky in my eyes when I straightened up, and it was blue and gold. I felt the weight of Meriem's head on my thigh. We stayed like that, half asleep, for a long time. When it got too hot, she stood up, and I followed her. I caught up with her, put my arm around her waist, and we walked together, like a single body. She smiled the whole time, dreamily, her eyes nearly closed. We reached the train station, still embracing. You could do that in those days. Not like today. While we were looking at each other with a new curiosity aroused by physical desire, she said, "I'm darker than you." I asked her if she could come back one evening. She laughed again and shook her head to say no. I dared to ask, "Do you want to marry me?" Her gulp of surprise was like a dagger in my heart. She hadn't been expecting that. I think she would have preferred to let our relationship continue as a source of natural amusement rather than become the prelude to a more serious engagement. Then she wanted to know if I loved her. I answered that I didn't know what that meant when I used words, but when I was silent, it became obvious in my head. You're smiling? Hmm, that means you understand...Yes, it's a big fib. From beginning to end. The scene's too perfect, I made it all up. Of course I never dared to say any such thing to Meriem. Her extravagant beauty, her disposition, and her assurance of a better life than mine always struck me dumb. Her type of woman has disappeared in this country today: free, brash, disobedient, aware of their body as a gift, not as a sin or a shame. The only time I saw a cold shadow come over her was when she told me about her domineering, polygamous father, whose lecherous eyes stirred up doubt and panic in her. Books delivered her from her family and offered her a pretext for getting away from Constantine; as soon as she could, she'd enrolled in the University of Algiers.

Meriem left around the end of summer, our romance had lasted only several weeks, and the day I realized she was gone forever I broke every dish in the house, insulting Mama and Musa and all the world's victims. Anger blurred my sight, but I remember Mama sitting calmly and watching me empty myself of my passion, serene and almost amused by her victory over all the women in the world. What followed was nothing but a long wrench of separation. Meriem wrote me letters that came to my office. I'd answer her with fury and anger. She'd describe her studies, the progress of her thesis, her tribulations as a rebellious student, but then everything gradually dwindled. Her letters became shorter and less frequent. Until one day they simply stopped altogether. All the same, I kept waiting for the Algiers bus at the train station, just to make myself suffer, for months and months.

Listen, I think this is the last get-together for you and me, go over there and insist that he join us. He'll come this time…

Bonjour, monsieur. You look as though you have Latin ancestry, nothing surprising about that in this town, which has given herself to sailors from all over the globe since the dawn of time. You're a teacher? No. Hey, Musa! Another bottle and some olives, please! What's this? The gentleman is deaf and dumb? Our guest doesn't speak any language? Is that true? He reads lips…Well, at least you know how to read. My young friend here has a book in which no one listens to anyone else. You should like it. It should be more interesting than your newspaper clippings, in any case.

What would you call a story that puts four characters around a table: a Kabyle waiter the size of a giant, an apparently tubercular deaf-mute, a young graduate student with a skeptical eye, and an old wine bibber who makes assertions but offers no proofs?

XV

I beg you to forgive this old man I've become. Which is itself a great mystery, by the way. These days, I'm so old that I often tell myself, on nights when multitudes of stars are sparkling in the sky, there must necessarily be something to be discovered from living so long. Living, what an effort! At the end, there must necessarily be, there has to be, some sort of essential revelation. It shocks me, this disproportion between my insignificance and the vastness of the cosmos. I often think there must be something all the same, something in the middle between my triviality and the universe!

But often enough I backslide, I start roaming the beach with a pistol in my fist, scouting around for the first Arab who looks like me so I can kill him. With my history, tell me, what else can I do but replay it over and over? Mama's still alive, but she's mute. We haven't spoken for years, and I content myself with drinking her coffee. The rest of the country is of no concern to me, except for the lemon tree, the beach, the bungalow, the sun, and the echo of the gunshot. And so I've lived this way a long time, like a sort of sleepwalker, shuttling between the offices where I've worked and my different residences. Some sketchy affairs with various women, a lot of exhaustion. No, nothing happened after Meriem left. I lived like the other people in the country, but with more discretion and more indifference. I watched the post-Independence enthusiasm consume itself and the illusions collapse, and then I started to get old, and now I'm sitting here in a bar, telling you this story that nobody ever tried to hear, except for Meriem and you, with a deaf-mute for a witness.

I've lived like a sort of ghost, observing the living as they bustle about in this big fishbowl. I've known the giddy feeling that comes with possessing an overwhelming secret, and that's how I've walked around, with a kind of endless monologue in my head. There have certainly been moments when I had a terrible urge to shout out to the world that I was Musa's brother and that we, Mama and I, were the only genuine heroes of that famous story, but who would have believed us? Who? What evidence could we offer? Two initials and a novel where no given name appears? The worst was when the packs of moon dogs started fighting and ripping one another apart to establish whether your hero had the same nationality as me or the people who shared his building. A fine joke! In the scuffle, nobody wondered what Musa's nationality was. He's referred to as the Arab, even by Arabs. Tell me, is that a nationality, "Arab"? And where's this country everybody claims to carry in their hearts, in their vitals, but which doesn't exist anywhere?

I went to Algiers a few times. Nobody talks about us, about my brother or Mama or me. Nobody! Our grotesque capital city, exposing its entrails to the open air, seemed like the worst of all the insults hurled at that unpunished crime. Millions of Meursaults, piled on top of one another, confined between a dirty beach and a mountain, dazed by murder and sleep, colliding with one another for lack of space. God, how I loathe the city of Algiers, the monstrous chewing sound it makes, its stench of rotten vegetables and rancid oil! It doesn't have a bay, it has jaws. And its waters won't be returning my brother's body to me, that's for sure! Once you've seen that city from the back, you can understand why the crime was perfect. And so I see them everywhere, your Meursaults, even in my apartment building here in Oran. Facing my balcony, just behind the last building on the outskirts of the city, there's an imposing mosque standing unfinished, like thousands of others in this country. I often look out at it from my window, and I loathe its architecture, the big finger pointed at the sky, the concrete still gaping. I also loathe the imam, who looks at his flock as if he's the steward of some kingdom. The hideous minaret makes me itch to speak some absolute blasphemy, something along the lines of "I will not prostrate myself before your pile of clay," and to repeat it in the wake of Iblis, the devil himself…Sometimes I'm tempted to climb up that prayer tower, reach the level where the loudspeakers are hung, lock myself in, and belt out my widest assortment of invective and sacrilege. I long to list my impieties in detail. To bellow that I don't pray, I don't do my ablutions, I don't fast, I will never go on any pilgrimage, and I drink wine—and what's more, the air that makes it better. To cry out that I'm free, and that God is a question, not an answer, and that I want to meet him alone, at my death as at my birth.

After your hero was sentenced to die, a priest visited him in his cell; in my case, there's a whole pack of religious fanatics hounding me, trying to convince me that

the stones of this country don't only sweat with suffering, and that God is watching over us. I should shout out
to them, say I've been looking at those unfinished walls
for years, there isn't anything or anyone in the world I
know better. Maybe at one time, way back, I was able to
catch a glimpse of the divine order. The face I saw was as
bright as the sun and the flame of desire — and it belonged
to Meriem. I tried to find it again. In vain. Now it's all
over. Can you imagine the scene? Me bawling into the
microphone while they scramble to break down the door
of the minaret so they can stop my mouth. They try to
make me listen to reason, they're distraught, they tell me
there's another life after death. And I answer them and
say, "A life where I can remember this one!" And then I
die, maybe stoned to death, but with the mic in my hand,
me, Harun, brother of Musa, son of the vanished father.
Ah, the martyr's grand gesture! Crying out his naked
truth. You live elsewhere, you can't imagine what an old
man has to put up with when he doesn't believe in God,
doesn't go to the mosque, has neither wife nor children,
and parades his freedom around like a provocation.

One day the imam tried to talk to me about God, telling me I was old and should at least pray like the others,
but I went up to him and made an attempt to explain that I
had so little time left, I didn't want to waste it on God. He
tried to change the subject by asking me why I was calling him "Monsieur" and not "El-Sheikh." That got me
mad, and I told him he wasn't my guide, he wasn't even
on my side. "Yes, my son," he said, putting his hand on
my shoulder, "I am on your side. But you have no way of
knowing it, because your heart is blind. I shall pray for

you." Then, I don't know why, but something inside me snapped. I started yelling at the top of my lungs, and I insulted him and said I wouldn't put up with being prayed for by him. I grabbed him by the collar of his gandoura. I poured out on him everything that was in my heart, joy and anger together. He seemed so sure of himself, didn't he? And yet none of his certainties was worth one hair on the head of the woman I loved. He wasn't even sure he was alive, because he was living like a dead man. I might look as if I was the one who'd come up empty-handed, but I was sure about me, about everything, sure of my life and sure of the death I had waiting for me. Yes, that was all I had. But at least I had as much of a hold on it as it had on me. I had been right, I was still right, I would always be right. It was as if I had always been waiting for this moment and for the first light of this dawn to be vindicated. Nothing, nothing mattered, and I knew why. So did he. Throughout the whole absurd life I'd lived, a dark wind had been rising toward me from somewhere deep in my future. What did other people's deaths or a mother's love matter to me; what did his God or the lives people choose or the fate they think they elect matter to me when we're all elected by the same fate, me and billions of privileged people like him who also called themselves my brothers? Couldn't he see, couldn't he see that? Everybody was privileged. There were only privileged people. The others would all be condemned one day. And he'll be condemned too, if the world's still alive. What would it matter if he were accused of murder and then executed because he didn't cry at his mother's funeral, or if I were accused of having killed a man on July 5, 1962, and not one day sooner? Salamano's dog was worth just as much as his wife. The little robot woman was just as guilty as the Parisian woman Masson married, or as Marie, who had wanted me to marry her. What did it matter that Meriem now offered her lips to another man? Couldn't he, couldn't this condemned man see that from somewhere deep in my future...All the shouting had me gasping for air. But they were already tearing the imam from my grip and a thousand arms wrapped themselves around me and brought me under control. The imam calmed them, though, and looked at me for a moment without saying anything. His eyes were full of tears. Then he turned and disappeared.

If I believe in God? Don't make me laugh! After all the hours we've spent together...I don't know why every time someone has a question about the existence of God he turns to man and waits for the answer. Ask *him* the question, put it directly to *him*! Sometimes I have the feeling I'm really inside that minaret, and I hear them out there, determined to break down the door I've locked so well, howling to wake the dead for my death. There they are, just on the other side, drooling with rage. You hear that door cracking? Tell me, do you hear it? I do. It's about to give way. And you know what I shout back at them? It's a single sentence nobody understands: "There's no one here! There has never been anyone! The mosque is empty, the minaret is empty. It's emptiness itself!" And for sure, there will be a large crowd of spectators the day of my execution and they will greet me with cries of hate. Maybe your hero was right from the beginning: There was never any survivor in that story. Everybody died all at once, all at the same time.

Mama's still alive today, but what's the point? She says practically nothing. And for my part, I talk too much, I think. It's the great shortcoming in murderers no one has punished yet, as your writer seems to have known all too well...Ah! Just one last joke, of my own invention. Do you know how "Meursault" is pronounced in Arabic? You don't? *El-Merssoul.* "The envoy," or "the messenger." Not bad, eh? Well, right, right, this time I really must stop. The bar's going to close, and everyone's waiting for us to empty our glasses. To think that the sole witness of our meeting is a deaf-mute whose only pleasures are cutting up newspapers and smoking cigarettes! My God, how you love to make fun of your creatures...

Do you find my story suitable? It's all I can offer you. It's my word. I'm Musa's brother or nobody's. Just a compulsive liar you met with so you could fill up your notebooks...It's your choice, my friend. It's like the biography of God. Ha, ha! No one has ever met him, not even Musa, and no one knows if his story is true or not. The Arab's the Arab, God's God. No name, no initials. Blue overalls and blue sky. Two unknown persons on an endless beach. Which is truer? An intimate question. It's up to you to decide. *El-Merssoul!* Ha, ha.

I too would wish them to be legion, my spectators, and savage in their hate.

KAMEL DAOUD is an Algerian journalist based in Oran, where he writes for the *Quotidien d'Oran* — the third largest French-language Algerian newspaper. His articles have appeared in *Libération*, *Le Monde*, and *Courrier International*, and are regularly reprinted around the world. A finalist for the Prix Goncourt, *The Meursault Investigation* won the Prix François Mauriac and the Prix des Cinq-Continents de la francophonie. International rights to the novel have been sold in twenty countries. A dramatic adaptation of *The Meursault Investigation* will be performed at the 2015 Festival d'Avignon, and a feature film is slated for release in 2017.

JOHN CULLEN is the translator of many books from Spanish, French, German, and Italian, including Yasmina Khadra's Middle East Trilogy (*The Swallows of Kabul*, *The Attack*, and *The Sirens of Baghdad*), Eduardo Sacheri's *The Secret in Their Eyes*, Yasmina Reza's *Happy Are the Happy*, and Chantal Thomas's *The Exchange of Princesses*. He lives in upstate New York.